# Three Sisters Flew Home

MARY FITT

*With an introduction by Curtis Evans*

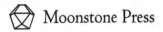 Moonstone Press

This edition published in 2022 by Moonstone Press
www.moonstonepress.co.uk

Introduction © 2022 Curtis Evans
Originally published in 1936 by Nicholson and Watson Ltd
*Three Sisters Flew Home* © the Estate of Kathleen Freeman, writing as Mary Fitt

The right of Kathleen Freeman to be identified as author of this work has been
asserted in accordance with the Copyright, Designs and Patents Act 1988

ISBN 978-1-899000-58-6
eISBN 978-1-899000-59-3

A CIP catalogue record for this book is available from the British Library

Text designed and typeset by Tetragon, London
Cover illustration by Jason Anscomb
Printed and bound by CPI Group (UK) Ltd, Croydon, CR0 4YY

# Contents

# INTRODUCTION

Although Kathleen Freeman was no neophyte novelist when she published, in 1936, at nearly forty years of age, her first 'Mary Fitt' mystery, *Three Sisters Flew Home*, she was at that time merely an initiate in fictional murder. Despite her lack of experience as a crime writer, however, Mary Fitt (as we will call her) scored a critical and popular success with her debut mystery that many of her more experienced colleagues might well have envied. With *Three Sisters Flew Home* the author launched a prosperous and lauded career as a mystery writer that lasted nearly a quarter of a century, until her untimely death in 1959 at the age of sixty-one.

With their initial murder essays even some of the crime-fiction genre's most esteemed authors tended to play it safe, like Ngaio Marsh, who has long been deemed one of the members of that killer quartet known as England's 'Queens of Crime' (composed of Marsh, Margery Allingham, Agatha Christie and Dorothy L. Sayers), although in fact Marsh was a native New Zealander. In her first stab at murder, the detective novel *A Man Lay Dead*, which was published but a couple of years before *Three Sisters Flew Home*, Marsh could not have made her criminous setting more classical: the act of fatal violence takes place at a country-house party, ironically during a game of 'murder'. The murder game, as it is called in *A Man Lay Dead*, or 'murder-party', as it is dubbed in *Three Sisters Flew Home*, was in great vogue between the First and the Second World War, when death — which had been, and soon would become again, all too real — had its sting rendered harmless by being turned into a jovial party amusement, like charades, musical chairs, scavenger hunts or hide-and-seek.

In the simplest form of the murder game, as we see it in *Three Sisters Flew Home*, players draw lots to see who plays the murderer, the corpse and the detective. The detective waits while the lights are turned out and the players scatter. Then the murderer 'tags' a victim by placing his or her hands around the victim's neck. This lucky person then waits ten seconds, screams and falls down 'dead'. The lights go on, the surviving players gather in the drawing room or what have you, and the detective through rounds of questioning attempts to determine whodunit. In more elaborate versions of the game, a full mock trial is said to have followed!

According to contemporary newspapers, the first murder-party was arranged by renowned American society hostess (that is, professional party planner) Elsa Maxwell, who by her own admission had cribbed the murder game from American illustrator Neysa McMein, a member of the Algonquin Round Table, an informal club of New York City culture mavens. Inspired by the infamous 1927 Snyder–Gray murder case, which she had covered in the press, McMein devised 'murder' not long afterwards. Other parlour games this ingenious woman concocted during the frivolous years of the Roaring Twenties included 'market place', 'books' and 'sex appeal'.

The first and most famous murder-party that Elsa Maxwell planned took place in London in May 1930, at the fabulous St James's Place mansion of wealthy American-born Ava Lowle Willing Astor Lister, aka Ava, Lady Ribblesdale, former wife of American plutocrat John Jacob Astor IV, who went down with the *Titanic*, and widow of late English Liberal politician Thomas Lister, 4th Baron Ribblesdale. 'Realizing that the world is full of amateur sleuths, each one of whom knows exactly how every murder mystery may be solved,' the widely syndicated features columnist Joan

Littlefield pertly reported in her 'Notes from London' column, 'Lady Ribblesdale decided to give a "murder-party," in order that some of her friends might have a chance to prove what they could do when confronted with the scene of a horrid deed "perpetrated" in her house.' In contrast with Lady Macbeth, Lady Ribblesdale just wanted her guests to have fun – and to make sure to tell all their friends about it.

'Twenty-five guests pretended that a twenty-sixth, a young girl, had been murdered and all started hunting for clues. They finally convicted the Duke of Marlborough of the "murder",' reported influential American newspaper editor and columnist Arthur Brisbane of Lady Ribblesdale's do, before adding dourly, though no doubt accurately:

> In this country, it is not necessary to make murder a game, it is a solemn reality. In Buffalo, not long ago, young people sat at dinner. Strangers entered, masked. One guest, thinking it a joke, tried to tear a mask from one of the hidden faces, and was knocked under the table. Three hundred thousand dollars' worth of jewelry was taken.

Who had need of the Duke of Marlborough as a cod criminal, in other words, in a country which had been literally bullet-riddled by the likes of John Dillinger, Ma Barker, Bonnie and Clyde, and Al Capone, not to mention a horde of lesser hoods?

Not one to be outdone by ambitious aristocratic rivals or shamed by the disapproval of press bluenoses who deemed murder no joke, a few months later the colourful Isabel, Lady Chaytor, wife of Sir Edmund Chaytor, 6th Baronet of Croft and Witton Castle, atmospherically staged a murder-party in 'the dungeons of Witton Castle', her husband's family seat in County Durham. After departing the dungeons, her surviving guests cosily reassembled to elucidate the crime 'at a nearby inn where sausages and beer awaited them'. (Whether Elsa Maxwell planned this affair as well is unclear.) The next year, Lady Chaytor, perhaps bored with 'balls, whacky parties, charity dos, speeches, a jaunt across the Syrian desert and the odd car accident', set off for Australia with her much younger male pilot in a Gipsy Moth biplane to lecture to the people of that country on the latest trends in European fashion.

Bloody murder had become but the latest thing among England's fashionable set, but what of the United States, rife with gangsters and gun molls? Arthur Brisbane's grim pronouncement notwithstanding, the murder game, or variations of it, was soon being gaily played at parties all across America. In 1931 it was said to have 'swept like an epidemic over the beach and country colonies of Long Island', while among a more modest coterie at the coastal town of Tarpon Springs, Florida, Miss Janet Sage, a twenty-one-year-old music teacher and daughter of a real-estate broker, held a costume murder-party at her home, with guests drolly 'garbed as apache dancers, gypsies, detectives, gunmen and Chinamen'. A bespectacled twenty-year-old local florist memorably named Jewel Millard Curry won the prize for best costume, having wowed the assembly with his appearance as British thriller writer Sax Rohmer's fiendish Asian criminal mastermind, Dr Fu Manchu. Dinner was given after the conclusion of the case and consisted of 'prison rations', served cafeteria-style and consumed while seated on the floor. Out in California the next year, actress Una Merkel, who played shamus Sam Spade's loyal secretary Effie Perine in the 1931 adaptation of Dashiell Hammett's hard-boiled detective novel *The Maltese Falcon*, held a swanky murder-party at her Hollywood domicile, with comic actor Andy Devine taking the part of the district attorney, to the company's vast delight.

Jolly murder-parties continued to afford measures of amusement during the depths of the Great Depression, even as rumours of another world war began increasingly to resound. In 1937, Elsa Maxwell, at it yet again, nearly caused an international incident in Fascist Italy – or so she herself, to much newspaper publicity, claimed – with an ingenious (or possibly over-ingenious) murder-party that she had devised in Rome. This game included a brace of fictitious threatening letters, which unfortunately drew the anxious attention of humourless Italian policemen, who had not been let in on Maxwell's little joke and feared that some form of forbidden skullduggery was running afoot in the Eternal City.

One real-life murder-party bizarrely converged with actual crime in England during the winter of 1934–35, when John Stephenson Bainbridge, a youthful private on Christmas leave from the Durham Light Infantry, was arrested, tried, convicted and executed for murdering, at his home in the town of Bishop Auckland, Edward Frederick Herdman, an elderly solicitor's clerk, former lay Methodist minister and well-known local historian and collector of communion tokens, whom Bainbridge had called upon on New Year's Eve to draw up his will. On her return to the house, Herdman's daughter discovered to her horror her father dead in the dining room; he had been bludgeoned with a fireplace poker and his throat had been severed with a pocketknife. Adding an odd dollop of irresistible irony for the press, after Bainbridge had departed Herdman's house earlier in the evening, ostensibly leaving the old man in good health, he had attended a New Year's Eve party with his fiancée at Gateshead, where he took part in a murder game, drawing the ominous ace of spades from a pack of cards and thereby being assigned the role of murderer! Evidently Bainbridge committed two murders in one night, once in jest and once in all-too-deadly earnest.

Naturally, mystery writers in the thirties, ever on the lookout for narsty novelties, employed the popular pastime of murder as a sort of meta plot device in their own criminal fictions. Ngaio Marsh later recalled that she had actually begun writing *A Man Lay Dead* in 1931, three years before it was published, on a dismal wet Sunday in her basement flat, not long after having read about the murder game in the society columns of London newspapers. How pleasant it must have been for the socially ambitious Marsh, on that depressing grey day in her dreary dwelling, to escape vicariously, like a much desired guest, into a posh country-house murder-party like those thrown by Ladies Ribblesdale and Chaytor! 'That was the season, in England, when the Murder Game was popular at weekend parties,' Marsh recalled several decades later. 'I thought it might be an idea for a whodunit… if a real corpse was found instead of a phoney one. Luckily for me, as it turned out, I wasn't aware until much later that a French practitioner had been struck with the same notion.'

The 'French practitioner' to whom Marsh alluded was Henry Bordeaux, whose sole essay in detection, forthrightly entitled even in its French edition *Murder Party* (1931), told of lovely film star Clarisse Villevert, who, after having been selected to play the 'corpse' at the murder game devised by the American-born wife of the Comte de Foix, is discovered dead in fact, to the horror of the other guests of the affair. Bordeaux dedicated the novel to a charming American in Paris, Elsie de Wolfe, Lady Mendl, platonic wife of British diplomat Sir Charles Mendl, Lady Mendl having introduced the murder-party game to the City of Light.

The same year in which Henry Bordeaux's novel appeared in France, where it created a 'tremendous sensation', it was translated into English and published in the United States and the United Kingdom. In both Anglophone countries it received rave reviews from a coven of crime-fiction critics, including none other than E. C. Bentley, president of England's Detection Club and the author of the landmark detective novel *Trent's Last Case*. Another murder-party mystery, one not alluded to by Ngaio Marsh, was serialized that same year and published as a novel on both sides of the Atlantic in 1932: Roland Pertwee and John Hastings Turner's *It Means Mischief*, in which Lord Studholme, a 'thoroughly vicious' press baron (is there any other kind in vintage crime fiction?), is slain for real at a murder-party where he had been the designated victim. (Although he was an accomplished playwright, director, novelist, screenwriter and actor who made a not insignificant contribution to crime fiction, Roland Pertwee is best known today as the father of actor Jon Pertwee, who portrayed British television's beloved sci-fi hero Doctor Who for five years during the Swinging Seventies.) Yet another 1931 mystery that made use of the murder-party plot device – and another that Ngaio Marsh neglected to mention – was popular American author Ben Ames Williams's *An End to Mirth*, in which jokester Hollywood film producer Ned Brace elects to play the corpse during the murder game he has staged and ends up – you will have guessed it by now – actually dead. Williams later published the novel *Leave Her to Heaven* (1944), which was made into the classic noirish film of the same title starring actress Gene Tierney.

Thus, when *A Man Lay Dead* belatedly appeared in the UK in 1934, after having been accepted by publisher Geoffrey Bles, the murder game had been previously played in at least a trio of other novels. Indeed, in just 1934 alone, murder-parties served as the bases for the plots not only of Marsh's novel but of the play *Murder Party* by Irish playwright Falkland Cary, and the British film *The Night of the Party* (aka *The Murder Party*), a so-called 'quota quickie' mystery thriller based on the Pertwee–Turner novel that starred

Leslie Banks, Jane Baxter and Ernest Thesiger and was directed by Michael Powell, later renowned for such classic post-war films as *Black Narcissus*, *The Red Shoes* and *Peeping Tom*. Then, in 1935, British author E. Charles Vivian published *Seventeen Cards*, one in his series of Inspector Head mysteries, wherein yet another genuine murder-party murder takes place at a country mansion, this one, in another classic crime-fiction trope, isolated from the rest of the world by a sudden snowstorm.

So, by 1936, when Mary Fitt's *Three Sisters Flew Home* was published in the UK by Ivor Nicholson and the United States by Doubleday, Doran, murder-party murders had appeared in at least five novels, a play and a film based on one of the novels. (Doubtlessly there were more such works, too.) Although in the estimation of jaded mystery reviewers the plot device had become hackneyed by this point, the brilliant and original usage which Mary Fitt made of it in her impressive debut novel brought the murder game breathtakingly to life again, like the legendary animated ivory statue Galatea; and critics, reminiscent of the legendary sculptor Pygmalion, promptly fell in love with Fitt's dazzling creation.

\*

As a classical scholar in her 'day job' at a Welsh university, Mary Fitt unsurprisingly approached the crime novel in a classic manner, frequently staging her books at country houses and even formal, full-dress country-house parties – see the recently reprinted *Death on Herons' Mere* – and *Three Sisters Flew Home* is no exception. The novel takes place during a few hours of a house party held on New Year's Eve at the country manor of Claribel Lorimer, a supremely selfish sculptor who specializes, appropriately enough given her duplicitous, self-serving and self-deluding nature, in the design of masks. As the author cuttingly puts it: 'it was her great gift that, though she herself acknowledged no laws of conduct, she could always think of those that applied to other people; and it never took her a moment to convince herself that she was right.'

The guests at Claribel's New Year's parties invariably consist greatly of her discarded, current and intended lovers, these being on this occasion sardonic Cretan pianist and composer John Markakis (who reflects that had Claribel been a Minoan princess, the locals would have thrown her to the Minotaur); sylvan-landscape painter John Carraway; sensitive poet Paul Sylens; he-man explorer Marcus Praed; and, Claribel's current quarry, an ingenuous young actor by the name of Desmond. Then there are, just for 'cover', a couple of Claribel's seemingly inconsequential art-student protégées, Betty and Peggy (I do not believe we ever learn their surnames), a certain nameless dark Irishman who steps on Betty's toes during dances and an inconsequential couple named George and Dione. Far more significantly, there is also an intriguing trio of captivating, lovely young sisters who go by the names of Ursula, Theresa and Lucy, who are Claribel's special guests for the evening, though they plan to exit the party early to board their plane and return whence they came (wherever this may be exactly). Last and least there is Gilbert Lorimer, Claribel's compliant, cuckolded husband, who at this latest of Claribel's festivities is seemingly as helpful and as negligible to his fickle spouse as ever.

The whole of this elegantly economical novel is devoted to detailing the animosities that develop and deepen dangerously over the course of several hours at the party, as the guests dance and play the murder game not once or twice but three times. Finally, the compelling closing pages take us – after a certain ceremonial dagger has wended its way like an evil charm among the guests – to meet murder (the real thing). 'Yes. I can feel it too – the alarm, the fear you speak of,' observes the eldest and most judicious of the three sisters, Ursula, to the painter John Carraway. 'There is an influence at work in this house, a disintegrating one.' At a later point, even Claribel herself realizes, to her baffled consternation, that 'in this house, which she had thought filled with her friends, she was surrounded by enemies... For the first time in her experience, Claribel was aware that the situation was out of her control.'

Is it the beguiling sisters who are actually in control of events at Claribel's party? The author compares the strange women to the 'three choric Graces', the Charites, Greek goddesses of charm, beauty, creativity, fecundity. Yet are they more like the three Fates, the Moirai Clotho, Lachesis and Atropos, Greek goddesses of destiny? Readers may be reminded of Agatha Christie's impressive late Miss Marple detective novel *Nemesis* (1971) and its trio of weird sisters Clotilde, Lavinia and Anthea, although *Nemesis* and *Sisters* are rather different animals. Reviewers of contemporary and recent vintage alike have compared *Three Sisters Flew Home* to fairy stories, with blogger Kate Jackson observing in 2019, for example, that the novel has a 'fairy-tale quality', what with its 'night-time setting' at a party and the way in which each of the sisters seems to attach herself 'to a male guest', which to me is suggestive of Cinderella having to depart the prince's elegant ball before her fairy godmother's wondrous enchantment expires at midnight.

What would happen were the sisters to tarry too long at Claribel's New Year's party? Why did Claribel invite them in the first place, and why did they accept her invitation? The novel's strange romantic quality becomes more pronounced as readers scent (or imagine that they do) a delicately exotic whiff of those strife-ridden fictional Balkan kingdoms Ruritania and Graustark – as described in the work of Anthony Hope and George Barr McCutcheon, respectively – not to mention Agatha Christie's own Herzoslovakia, which plays such a prominent role in her parodic 1925 spy thriller *The Secret of Chimneys*; yet the romance in *Sisters* is a dark one at its heart.

Make no mistake about it, *Sisters* is a thriller, although more of a psychological one, plunging into deep, dark mental waters with its characters as the hands of the clock tick ominously towards midnight and the putatively festive occasion turns increasingly sinister. It is a novel which could have made a gripping Alfred Hitchcock film, had even Hitch been able to capture its rare elusive qualities. Certainly critics, eager for something new in murder fiction, discerned novelty in *Three Sisters Flew Home* and accordingly raved about the book, particularly in the UK, where Mary Fitt, like Gladys Mitchell, quickly gathered what might be termed a cult-like following. The English translator and poet Edward Powys Mathers – an eminent crime-fiction reviewer who adopted the inquisitorial pseudonym of 'Torquemada' and a designer of wickedly fiendish newspaper crosswords – positively swooned over *Sisters*, like a giddy bobby-soxer at a crooner's concert, writing from his seat at the *London Observer*:

> When I saw that Mary Fitt was about to give us a murder committed during the playing of the murder game, I quailed; the thing had been done so often. Now that I have finished 'Three Sisters Flew Home,' I confess that if its authoress chose to rewrite the dullest adventure of Sexton Blake or Rupert Bear [a character in a British children's comic strip], I would read and reread. As chapter after iridescent chapter passes of this book, your suspicion that such exquisite writing must be a fluke becomes lulled, then dissipated altogether, and you relax on to the assured beauty of the style as on to a bed of down. We are guided through the mazes of Claribel's party by a Vergil whose insight into the developed human soul is wise even to devastation.

More succinctly, yet no less praisefully, than the enraptured Torquemada, Richard Burleigh in the Birmingham *Sunday Mercury* wrote of the novel: 'A murder story told in exquisite prose and with characterization and interpretation that would grace a classic. A fascinating, beautiful "thriller".'

In the *Vancouver Province*, under the headline 'Improvement on Graustark', a certain 'T.S.' wrote enthusiastically of *Sisters*: 'The book is written with a police fidelity to detail and with considerable discrimination in the unfolding of character, but it depends for its ultimate success upon its created atmosphere. This, subtly suggested and delicately yet evenly sustained, makes it well worth reading.' In the *New York Times Book Review* the novel was honoured by being invited above stairs, in a manner of speaking, to receive its review in the company of respectable mainstream literature (albeit that 'in a lighter vein'), with humbler crime thrillers and detective fiction duly appearing 'in their proper place' down below. The enchanted anonymous reviewer pronounced of *Sisters*: 'Mary Fitt has written a quaint and curious story with a fantastic plot and the fidelity to detail of a detective thriller... The scheme of the novel is cleverly conceived... an unusual and oddly interesting attack on the murder theme.'

*Three Sisters Flew Home* was reprinted in the UK in a Penguin paperback edition in 1953, but for nearly seven full decades publishers did not favour mystery readers with additional return visits. Now, through the grace of Moonstone, vintage-mystery fans have the opportunity to read what their forebears in the thirties deemed one of the most unique – and uniquely appealing – fictions from the golden age of genteel murder.

## ABOUT THE AUTHOR

One of the prominent authors of the classical detective fiction of the Golden Age and afterwards was herself a classicist: Kathleen Freeman, a British lecturer in Greek at the University College of South Wales and Monmouthshire, Cardiff (now Cardiff University) between 1919 and 1946. Primarily under the pseudonym Mary Fitt, Freeman published twenty-nine crime novels between 1936 and 1960, the last of them posthumously. Eighteen of these novels are chronicles of the criminal investigations of her series sleuth, Superintendent Mallett of Scotland Yard, while the remaining eleven of them, nine of them published under the pseudonym Mary Fitt and one apiece published under the respective names of Stuart Mary Wick and Kathleen Freeman, are stand-alone mysteries, some of which are notable precursors of the modern psychological crime novel. There is also a single collection of Superintendent Mallett 'cat mystery' short stories, *The Man Who Shot Birds*.

From the publication of her lauded debut detective novel, *Three Sisters Flew Home*, Mary Fitt – like Gladys Mitchell, an author with whom in England she for many years shared the distinguished publisher Michael Joseph – was deemed a crime writer for 'connoisseurs'. Within a few years, Fitt's first English publisher, Ivor Nicholson & Watson, proudly dubbed her devoted following a 'literary cult'. In what was an unusual action for the time, Nicholson & Watson placed on the dust jacket of their edition of Fitt's *Death at Dancing Stones* (1939) accolades from such distinguished, mystery-writing Fitt fans as Margery Allingham ('A fine detective story and a most ingenious puzzle'), Freeman Wills Crofts ('I should like to offer her my congratulations') and J. J. Connington ('This is the best book by Miss Mary Fitt I have yet read').

If not a crowned 'queen of crime' like Allingham, Agatha Christie, Dorothy L. Sayers and Ngaio Marsh, Kathleen Freeman in her Mary Fitt guise was, shall we say, a priestess of peccadillos. In 1950 Freeman was elected to the prestigious Detection Club, a year after her crime-writing cover was blown in the gossip column 'The Londoner's Diary' in the *Evening Standard*. Over the ensuing decade several of the older Mary Fitt mysteries were reprinted in paperback by Penguin and other publishers, while new ones continued to appear, to a chorus of praise from such keen critics of the crime-fiction genre as Edmund Crispin, Anthony Berkeley Cox (who wrote as, among others, Francis Iles) and Maurice Richardson. 'It is easy to run out of superlatives in writing of Mary Fitt,' declared the magazine *Queen*, 'who is without doubt among the first of our literary criminographers.'

Admittedly, Freeman enjoyed less success as a crime writer in the United States, where only ten of her twenty-nine mystery novels were published during her lifetime. However, one of Fitt's warmest boosters was the *New York Times*'s Anthony Boucher, for two decades the perceptive dean of American crime-fiction reviewers. In 1962, three years after Fitt's death, Boucher selected the author's 1950 novel *Pity for Pamela* for inclusion in the 'Collier Mystery Classics' series. In his introduction to the novel, Boucher lauded Fitt as an early and important exponent of psychological suspense in crime fiction.

Despite all the acclaim which the Mary Fitt mysteries formerly enjoyed, after Freeman's untimely death from congestive heart failure in 1959 at the age of sixty-one, the books, with very few exceptions – *Mizmaze* (Penguin, 1961), *Pity for Pamela* (Collier, 1962), *Death and the Pleasant Voices* (Dover, 1984) – fell almost entirely out of print.

Therefore, this latest series of sparkling reissues from Moonstone is a welcome event indeed for lovers of vintage British mystery, of which Kathleen Freeman surely is one of the most beguiling practitioners.

*

A native Midlander, Kathleen Freeman was born at the parish of Yardley near Birmingham on 22 June 1897. The only child of Charles Henry Freeman and his wife Catherine Mawdesley, Kathleen grew up and would spend most of her adult life in Cardiff, where she moved with her parents not long after the turn of the century. Her father worked as a brewer's traveller, an occupation he had assumed possibly on account of an imperative need to support his mother and two unmarried sisters after the death of his own father, a schoolmaster and clergyman without a living who had passed away at the age of fifty-seven. This was in 1885, a dozen years before Kathleen was born, but presumably the elder Charles Freeman bequeathed a love of learning to his family, including his yet-unborn granddaughter. Catherine Mawdesley's father was James Mawdesley, of the English seaside resort town of Southport, not far from Liverpool. James had inherited his father's 'spacious and handsome silk mercer's and general draper's establishment', impressively gaslit and 'in no degree inferior, as to amplitude, variety and elegance of stock, to any similar establishment in the metropolis or inland towns' (in the words of an 1852 guide to Southport), yet he died at the age of thirty-five, leaving behind a widow and three young daughters.

As a teenager, Kathleen Freeman was educated at Cardiff High School, which, recalling the 1930s, the late memoirist Ron Warburton remembered as 'a large attractive building with a large schoolyard in front, which had a boundary wall between it and the

pavement'. The girls attended classes on the ground floor, while
the boys marched up to the first (respectively, the first and second
floors in American terminology). 'The first-floor windows were
frosted so that the boys could not look down at the girls in the school
playground,' Warburton wryly recalled. During the years of the
Great War, Freeman, who was apparently an autodidact in ancient
Greek (a subject unavailable at Cardiff High School, although
the boys learned Latin), attended the co-educational, 'red-brick'
University College of South Wales and Monmouthshire, founded
three decades earlier in 1883, whence she graduated with a BA in
Classics in 1918. The next year saw both her mother's untimely
passing at the age of fifty-two and her own appointment as a lecturer in Greek at her alma mater. In 1922, she received her MA; a
Doctor of Letters belatedly followed eighteen years later, in rec-
ognition of her scholarly articles and 1926 book *The Work and Life
of Solon*, about the ancient Athenian statesman. Between 1919 and
1926 Freeman was a junior colleague at University College of her
former teacher Gilbert Norwood, who happened to share her great
love of detective fiction, as did another prominent classical scholar,
Gilbert Murray, who not long before his death in 1957 informed
Freeman that he had long been a great admirer of Mary Fitt.

Freeman's rise in the field of higher education during the first
half of the twentieth century is particularly impressive given the
facts, which were then deemed disabling, of her sex and modest
family background as the daughter of a brewer's traveller, which
precluded the possibility of a prestigious Oxbridge education. 'A
man will do much for a woman who is his friend, but to be suspected
of being a brewer's traveller... was not pleasant,' observes the mor-
tified narrator of William Black's novel *A Princess of Thule* (1883),
anxious to correct this socially damning misimpression. Evidently
unashamed of her circumstances, however, Freeman evinced a

lifetime ambition to reach ordinary, everyday people with her work, eschewing perpetual confinement in academe's ivory tower.

Before turning to crime writing in 1936 under the alias of Mary Fitt, Freeman published five mainstream novels and a book of short stories, beginning with *Martin Hanner: A Comedy* (1926), a well-received academic novel about a (male) classics professor who teaches at a red-brick university in northern England. After the outbreak of the Second World War, while she was still employed at the university, Freeman, drawing on her classical education, published the patriotically themed *It Has All Happened Before: What the Greeks Thought of Their Nazis* (1941).* She also lectured British soldiers headed to the Mediterranean theatre of war on the terrain, customs and language of Greece, a country she had not merely read about but visited in the Thirties. During the cold war, when Freeman, passed over for promotion, had retired from teaching to devote herself to writing in a world confronted with yet another totalitarian menace, she returned to her inspirational theme, publishing *Fighting Words from the Greeks for Today's Struggle* (1952). Perhaps her most highly regarded layman-oriented work from this period is *Greek City-States* (1950), in which, notes scholar Eleanor Irwin, Freeman uses her 'uncanny eye for settings, as is often seen in her mysteries', to bring 'the city-states to life'. Freeman explicitly drew on her interests in both classicism and crime in her much-admired book *The Murder of Herodes and Other Trials from the Athenian Law Courts* (1946), which was effusively praised by the late Jacques Barzun, another distinguished academic mystery fancier, as 'a superb book for the [crime] connoisseur'.

In spite of her classical background, Kathleen Freeman derived her 'Mary Fitt' pseudonym – which she also employed to publish

---

* Under the heading of 'Dictators', Freeman quotes Solon: 'When a man has risen too high, it is not easy to check him after; now is the time to take heed of everything.' Timeless words indeed!

juvenile fiction, including a series of books about an intrepid young girl named Annabella – not from ancient Greece but from Elizabethan England, Eleanor Irwin has hypothesized, for the name bears resemblance to that of Mary Fitton, the English gentlewoman and maid of honour who is a candidate for the 'Dark Lady' of Shakespeare's queer-inflected sonnets. Irwin points out that Freeman's 'earliest literary publications were highly personal reflections on relationships in sonnet form'. The name also lends itself to a pun – 'Miss Fitt' – which it is likely the author deliberately intended, given her droll wit and nonconformity.

While Kathleen Freeman's first four detective novels, which appeared in 1936 and 1937, are stand-alones, her fifth essay in the form, *Sky-Rocket* (1938), introduces her burly, pipe-smoking, green-eyed, red-moustached series police detective, Superintendent Mallett, who is somewhat reminiscent of Agatha Christie's occasional sleuth Superintendent Battle. The two men not only share similar builds but have similarly symbolic surnames.

Joined initially by acerbic police surgeon Dr Jones and later by the imaginative Dr Dudley 'Dodo' Fitzbrown – the latter of whom, introduced in *Expected Death* (1938), soon supersedes Jones – Superintendent Mallett would dominate Mary Fitt's mystery output over the next two decades. Only after Freeman's heart condition grew perilously grave in 1954 does it seem that the author's interest in Mallett and Fitzbrown dwindled, with the pair appearing in only two of the five novels published between 1956 and 1960. Similarly diminished in her final years was Freeman's involvement with the activities of the Detection Club, into which she initially had thrown herself with considerable zeal. In the first half of the decade she had attended club dinners with her beloved life partner, Dr Liliane Marie Catherine Clopet, persuaded Welsh polymath Bertrand Russell, an omnivorous detective-fiction reader, to speak at one of the dinners, and wrote a BBC radio play, *A Death in the Blackout* (in which Dr Fitzbrown appears), with the proceeds from the play going to the club.

Presumably Kathleen Freeman met Liliane Clopet at the University College of South Wales and Monmouthshire, where Clopet registered as a student in 1919. Precisely when the couple began cohabiting is unclear, but by 1929 Freeman had dedicated the first of what would be many books to Clopet ('For L.M.C.C.'), and by the Thirties the pair resided at Lark's Rise, the jointly owned house – including a surgery for Clopet and her patients – that the couple had built in St Mellons, a Cardiff suburb. In the author's biography on the back of her Penguin mystery reprints, Freeman noted that a friend had described the home where she lived as 'your Italian-blue house', though she elaborated: 'It is not Italian, but it is blue – sky-blue.' There Freeman would pass away and Clopet would reside for many years afterwards.

Born on 13 December 1901 in Berwick-upon-Tweed in Northumberland, Liliane Clopet was one of three children of native Frenchman Aristide Bernard Clopet, a master mariner, and his English wife Charlotte Towerson, a farmer's daughter. Although Aristide became a naturalized British citizen, the Clopets maintained close connections with France. In 1942, during the Second World War, Liliane's only brother, Karl Victor Clopet – a master mariner like his father who for a dozen years had run a salvage tug in French Morocco – was smuggled by Allied forces from Casablanca to London, where he provided details of Moroccan ports, beaches and coastal defences, which were crucially important to the victory of the United States over Vichy French forces at the ensuing Battle of Port Lyautey.

Even more heroically (albeit tragically), Liliane's cousin Evelyne Clopet served with the French Resistance and was executed by the Nazis in 1944, after British forces had parachuted her into

France; at her death she was only twenty-two years old. In 1956, under another pseudonym (Caroline Cory), Kathleen Freeman published a novel set in wartime France, *Doctor Underground*, in which she drew on Evelyne's experiences. A couple of years earlier, Liliane Clopet herself had published a pseudonymous novel, *Doctor Dear*, in which she depicted a female physician's struggles with sexism among her colleagues and patients.

Kathleen Freeman, who was rather masculine-looking in both her youth and middle age (boyish in her twenties, she grew stouter over the years, wearing her hair short and donning heavy tweeds), produced no issue and at her death left her entire estate, valued at over £300,000 in today's money, to Liliane Clopet. In a letter to another correspondent she avowed: 'My books are my children and I love them dearly.' Admittedly, Freeman shared custody of her mysteries with that queer Miss Fitt, but surely she loved her criminally inclined offspring, too. I have no doubt that the author would be pleased to see these books back in print again after the passage of so many years. Readers of vintage mysteries, now eager to embrace the stylish and sophisticated country-house detective novels and psychological suspense tales of an earlier era, will doubtless be pleased as well.

CURTIS EVANS

# I

From the first, Claribel's party went well.

She had chosen to begin it at the extraordinary time of a quarter to four in the afternoon; and this certainly meant twelve hours' entertainment. But Claribel always said she liked too much of everything.

Her guests came. They came in time. They would not have done this for anybody but her. But they came to her dark house at the very time she told them to, because they knew that she had something to offer them, something surprising, delicious, worth while. When they had received her casual invitation, by telephone, by note or word of mouth or even by wire, each one of them knew that this was the summons that must be accepted at all costs, for New Year's Eve. If any of them had made a previous arrangement, this must be cancelled. And yet, there were some of them who didn't want to go… Perhaps these had been before, had seen other New Years in at Claribel's parties. Perhaps one or two of them had done this more than once, and knew that, so long as Claribel chose, in her casual last-minute way, to invite them, they would do it again.

Oh yes, there were always a few 'old friends' in these annual gatherings. The question *they* asked themselves, as they came into her dimly lighted room, was, who of their number was *not* there this time?…

But they came. For after all, there were always new friends too. More than that; there was always Expectancy: what are we here for, what will she provide?

It would have been interesting to have seen the face, or even into the mind, of each person invited, as he stood, perhaps, with the telephone receiver in his hand, or the newly opened note or telegram. Some, no doubt, smiled naively, with pleasure, with ready acceptance. Others looked thoughtful, and took time to answer, although they knew their answer was predetermined. One, at least, looked haggard all of a sudden, and dark. Claribel's ways of communication were carefully chosen, too: she knew full well when to use her voice, or her written word, and when to use an impersonal medium. Those who knew her well enough could have told, simply by knowing how the invitation had been delivered, the status of each guest in Claribel's mind.

At a quarter to four they were all assembling. Quite suddenly, the dark lane leading to Claribel's door became full of sound and light, as car after car swung round the corner, startling the river swans, and crawled humming into line. Claribel's husband was at the door, quietly welcoming; he helped the ladies out, and collected their wraps and showed them where to go; he showed the men where to put their cars. By four o'clock he had them all upstairs for Claribel; and he was handing round the cups of tea which he seemed also to have poured out for them. At any rate, Claribel did nothing. She leaned against the chimney-breast at the side of the immense hearth, and with a sweet smile on her lips, and a gleam in her eyes, surveyed the room.

It was a beautiful room, very long and low, with many-beamed ceiling. It glowed, richly and darkly, in the light of the pine logs, and there was a pleasant, not too heavy, scent that met one as one came up the steep, winding stairs. Claribel had had the luck to pick up this old house by the river, as she picked up everything, when she wanted it, and at the price she wished to pay. None of her friends thought of grudging it to her; they sighed a little, maybe, when they first heard the news – but it was Claribel's luck, belonging to her as truly as her eyes or her brain, and one realized that she did, in some obscure way, achieve what seemed to fall to her by an absurd favouritism of fortune. To have done the same, one would have had to *be* Claribel: one doubts whether any of her circle would have wished just that.

At the back of the room Claribel's Christmas tree still stood, waiting for the Epiphany, its candles partly burnt except where Gilbert had fixed new ones, and its green, silver and crimson balls each with a point of light, like the gleam in Claribel's eyes.

She spoke softly, welcoming one and all, giving to each her hand, her gentlest voice, her smile. She was, at this point, conventionally dressed, in an afternoon frock of boyish cut, and she looked very charming – sophisticated and young.

# 2

The room was like a Rembrandt picture. The guests sat, or stood, or leaned about; their faces more or less dimly illuminated, their bodies lost in shadow. They looked like masks suspended from the ceiling at varying heights; and this was oddly appropriate, for Claribel herself made masks, of bronze and marble and wood and stone, and some of these were hung on the walls. Several of them were of people in the room; and it titillated Claribel's rather brutal sense of humour to look from the mask to the real face just below it: for the real face was set and immobile, and the mask was given a spurious life by the shadow-play from the fire. Claribel cared deeply for the things she herself had made, and very little for anything else… Her thoughts went a step further, and were wondering whether it was illusion, or whether the real faces had, during the years between, grown more and more like the masks. The idea pleased her.

A little murmuring of conversation was arising here and there. Two or three of the old friends had met, and had started a conversation in a corner about Socrates: or rather, they had taken it up, actually from the very point where they had left it off last year. Claribel distinctly remembered… Well, there was no harm in that: if they got interested and absorbed to the point of forgetting that they were at a party, she could easily break up the group with an ironical word, or tell Gilbert to put a shattering rumba on the gramophone. Claribel, although on occasion she could talk a great deal, had a deep hatred of discussion, because it got so quickly out of hand – *her* hand.

And then, suddenly a *frisson* went round the room. Everyone pricked up an ear. The talkers looked up, startled. Even the two quite negligible though pretty young girls sitting on pouffes by the fire swung round and looked at Gilbert and then at Claribel. There was always a sprinkling of such young girls at Claribel's parties; for Claribel, though she collected, and kept, people of distinction, or who at least were 'serious' and real, with work to do, was not actually at all a good judge of human quality, and these makeweights, for whose presence no one in the company could account, were merely Claribel's false swans. One could allow her a few wide shots of this kind – for she herself at the time truly thought them interesting – in return for her many bull's-eyes. The puzzle was, how she could achieve such amazing extremes – how anyone with such a flair, a genius, for spotting the right people, could go at times so hopelessly, boringly wrong. But then, Claribel did not work by intelligence, nor by any clear, heaven-sent inspiration: she groped blindly, but purposively, and through stumblings and blunderings, which she ignored or scarcely noticed or at least instantly forgot, she reached her objective. She might not know when she had got hold of the wrong; but when her grasp closed on the right, then she was infallible. Meanwhile the pretty young girls were harmless, even mildly pleasing as ornaments. They decorated the floor at Claribel's feet...

Outside – it was now quite dark – there was undoubtedly a stir. A car had arrived: no one heard it, but a light flashed past the uncurtained windows, throwing on them a moving silhouette of bare twigs; and those who looked down saw the huge black car, that filled the narrow lane. They were able to watch, from above, the whole process: the black-liveried chauffeur, looking like a part of the machine he controlled, detaching himself like a robot and coming to the near door. He held it open.

The three sisters descended. For a moment they swirled together like three choric Graces as they conferred – they always conferred about the simplest trifle – and there was a rustle of laughter as they swirled out again, and made for Claribel's iron-studded door. Already the robot chauffeur was back in his seat, and the great car was slowly crawling in reverse out of the lane. It made no more sound than the humming of a powerful electric wireless set.

'It's the girls,' said Claribel. 'Do go, Gilbert, dear…' She had not moved to the window.

Gilbert's tall thin form was already threading its way towards the stairs. And meanwhile the door of the street opened. The three sisters were inside.

Then everybody knew what Claribel's party was about this time.

# 3

They had come into the room for a moment to greet Claribel; and the company looked on as at a play, while Claribel, blonde-headed and neat, stepped composedly down from the kerb, and the three sisters half-encircled her. They already wore their party frocks, and from under their short fur jackets their petal-like skirts flowed down to the toes of their satin shoes. Each wore a different colour: Ursula, the eldest, wore the colour called petunia, and Theresa, the youngest, wore lime-green, but Lucy had on her favourite shade of blue, the colour of certain cinerarias. Ursula and Theresa wore slippers that matched their frocks; but Lucy's slippers were cardinal red. It was a pleasure to see their satin toes peeping out from under the folds of their frocks, and it reminded everybody at once of the poem, and they felt gay and cheerful.

Claribel led them out, and from a distant bedroom it seemed as if one could still hear a faint murmur, a rustling... Gilbert, too, went out, after setting John Markakis down at the piano to play one of his own compositions. Markakis played the piece, quickly and roughly and loudly: he had played it many times before in that room, and he no longer expected to be listened to, as on that first occasion years ago, when he – with another – had been Claribel's surprise. He did not mind at all that the old reverence and awe had evaporated. In fact, he rather liked the sensation; he felt that it did him good, gave him a sense of proportion, reduced him to nor-mality. He did deeply desire to be 'normal'. His genius was purely musical, and though he could think and talk in music, he could not do either very well in words, so that he had been impressed by Claribel and a theory she happened to have when he first met her.

She had been reading a book, and she met Markakis at somebody else's party. She had long ago forgotten the book. But Markakis was at bottom a simple, trusting creature, and because the beautiful and intelligible arrangement of sounds came easily to him, he thought nothing of it; but he thought a great deal of all those who could express themselves in words, especially long words and winding clauses. He was still, four years later, pursuing Claribel's idea of normality, which was that everybody should give up trying to shine – everybody except herself of course, because she was naturally perfect to begin with and had no need to go in for any spiritual exercises.

So Markakis had striven hard to give up trying to make people listen to his music – for that would mean that they would admire and praise *him* as well as the music, and he would enjoy it and that would be all wrong. He had also, since he met Claribel, got rid of his great friend and admirer, the man who had encouraged him to shine, and insisted on his being attended to. So he was well on the way to becoming normal. The odd thing was, Claribel's interest in him seemed to have waned, at the same time and in direct proportion. He never asked himself why Claribel had singled him out in the first place...

So now he sat down and played his piece, roughly and rapidly; and then he played a mazurka of Chopin, softly and sadly; and then he broke into another of his own pieces, and by that time the company had got over their initial courtesy. There was a murmur of talk, and then gradually, as he played on, they forgot him – as he had, perversely, intended. There had been a time when no one would have breathed or stirred – when he would have leapt to his feet and crashed his hands on the keys if anyone had spoken. But that, said Claribel, was all a pose. He must play *purely*, not for success or fame, but for himself only... She had once said, 'Play for *me*.' Now, when he played, it was to fill a gap while she was out of the room.

Markakis played on. It was now safe to play quite softly; they did not stop. He could overhear:

'Who are they – do you know?'

'Their names are Ursula, Lucy, Theresa –' The surname he could not hear.

'Where do they come from? Where did Claribel lay hold of them?'

Nobody knew.

'What do they *do*?'

'They are rich,' said someone. 'They have oodles of money. They are here on a visit, Claribel says.'

'I believe,' said another voice, 'Ursula paints – or does she play? Or is it Lucy who does everything and the other two nothing? They all ride, anyway.' Someone had seen them out riding in the Row.

'Together?'

'Yes – together. They always do everything together.'

'They are not alike,' a man's voice said thoughtfully.

'No,' another answered. There was a pause, which Markakis filled with a lovely phrase of Mozart's. 'The one in lime-green – the youngest, I imagine – is the most beautiful. She is,' he added, after another pause, 'extremely beautiful.' Nobody denied this or assented.

'But I think,' said Sylens the poet, the translator of Pindar, 'I think the eldest is the most subtle.'

'Ah,' said a third voice – and this was the mild, pleasant painter of trees, John Carraway, 'but it is Lucy who has the best character.'

'What do you mean by that?' One after the other of them was drawn in. The women, too, began to talk. The three men, Sylens, Carraway, and that first voice, which had proclaimed the beauty of Theresa – these three voices now receded, took their place like instruments in a symphony as the whole orchestra gradually is called into life. What, thought Markakis – and he rejoiced in his humility – are poor, feeble, tentative melodies like mine compared with this rich human symphony swelling and growing around me out of nothing? It has the one thing I and my creation lack: it has purpose, it has meaning and direction. Claribel, not I, is the composer; in her absence, we set ourselves, each according to his gifts, to play out her theme. And what is it now? 'Who are the Three Sisters?' Unawares, he began shaping the question into a phrase of sound, altering it, turning it this way and that, improvising answers, rejecting them, playing the answers he had heard. 'Ursula – the cleverest; Theresa – most beautiful; but Lucy – the heart of gold.' He played each theme in turn, directly, and with variations. 'And they are always together.' He played that, too. 'Where did Claribel find them? What are they doing here?' He was completely lost, improvising, happy; he had even forgotten to wish that there were someone present who understood the language of sounds and could share in his pleasure and respond to it with understanding. The only one who could have done that was –

Conversation had ceased.

Claribel's voice came across the room clearly. 'Well, now, I think, if you are all ready, we will go downstairs and dance.' Everyone had risen. Markakis, not able to react so quickly, had scarcely taken his hands off the keys. But he had heard the sharp note in her voice, and it sang like a blow in his ears. A pity. However, he could remember the themes, and write them down if they were worth it. He got up, without resentment, and came, last of all, towards the door, where Claribel stood waiting. She had changed her frock for a cocktail suit with wide flowing black silk trousers.

'You'll dance?' she said to him. 'Don't if you don't want to – there is no need. We have men enough to go round.'

Markakis shook his head.

'Then,' she said eagerly, laying her hand on his arm, 'you'll put on records, Markakis dear?'

He nodded.

She looked at him, curiously and affectionately, a little puzzled, perhaps, by his expression – by the dull, heavy look in his eyes, which did not go with his smile. She wondered, not for the first time, if he took drugs or had some other secret vice that gave him that heavy-lidded look; and the smile – was it too fixed to be natural? But he went on smiling, and nodding at her, and she was reassured. She slid her hand, ruby-nailed, along his forearm before she released him, and hurried after the rest.

Markakis followed slowly, down the tortuous steep stairs.

# 4

And now they were in the lower room. This, too, was long and low and dark; there were large pieces of dark furniture, a sideboard, an oak table. A fire burned at both ends.

After all, it had been Claribel who had put on the first record, a slow waltz, which she was dancing now with her husband. She always gave the first dance to Gilbert, whose style was perfect and with whom naturally she was at her best. They danced as one; he held her supple body closely to him so that she bent a little backward at the waist, and their long black legs moved as if some unseen bond united them. Gilbert's face was dark and serious, intent on her; the first dance was still, to him, a precious privilege. Afterwards, he would go away and do his duty by the other ladies, keeping his eye on Claribel. He knew to a moment when to approach her, and when to leave her alone. If things were going well with her, then he would not be needed as a dancing partner for the rest of the evening. But at the slightest flicker of discontent on that smooth, young, smiling face – Claribel was thirty-three years old, and looked eighteen – he would be instantly at her side, and she would be in his arms... Slowly, with long strides and beautifully timed hesitations, they traversed the length of the room. The others watched them.

Claribel half closed her eyes. She knew the importance of the first dance, before the rest of the company had quite made up their minds to take the floor. It was her exhibition dance. In another minute the music would have fired the others, got into their brains and filled their limbs with the rhythmic urge... She could not have trusted Markakis to choose the right record... He stood now by the gramophone, waiting to replace the waltz by something of his own choice. He held a black disk in one hand, and with the other was idly sifting the pile...

The three sisters sat together on an oak settle near the fireplace. The light in the angle of the wall seemed to pick them out in all their gay colours; their bracelets tinkled, Ursula's necklace of brilliants glittered kaleidoscopically, and with them, a faint new perfume had entered the room. They still wore their short jackets of fur, which was wise of them, for Claribel's house, in spite of all the fires, was full of cold draughts: it was old, and there was a penetrating wind outside.

Just before the record ended, two men got up simultaneously and came towards them. They stood together, bowing before the three sisters; John Carraway, the painter, was asking Ursula to dance, and Sylens, the poet, was requiring the same honour of Theresa. The lovely young girl was the first to rise, and as she quietly came to him, and gave him her hand, and allowed him to steer her away, it was to him as if a million birds had suddenly burst out singing. 'Everyone suddenly burst out singing, And I was filled with such delight –' It had been said already; there was nothing more to say. Yes, another poet had said it; and Sylens was not envious. What did it matter who got the credit, so long as beauty, supreme beauty, was created for all to see or hear, and to worship? He looked down at the magnolia-pale perfectly modelled face, the hazel-green eyes that looked out composedly across his shoulder; and he was staggered at the convention of ball-room dancing, which allows you to go up to a woman you admire or desire, and for a little space of time hold her to you, as it were, against all the world... Sylens did not believe in possessiveness; he held the view that beauty was too rare, too precious, not to be shared. And so he knew how to appreciate the brief moments when he too came into his own; but he knew also the pain of relinquishment. And like all poets he was haunted by the grief – not the fear – of death.

Should he speak to her? He knew exactly what her voice would be like – low and slow and composed. He did not think her character complex, or her experience wide – she was so young, surely not more than seventeen? Why should they talk? She would not have anything to say that he didn't know. She was not stupid; such beauty could not be. True beauty is never merely physical. When the record stopped, perhaps – But he must make up his mind! The record was ending! If he did not hurry and decide, she would leave him, go back into the circle of her sisters, and be lost for, oh such a long while – several dances. Where could they go, to talk? For of course they must talk – he must make her. He must find the secret of that amazing, still, yet intensely living beauty, before it faded like a dream out of his life again. Often he had felt this desire, this passionate clutching at the veil of the Mystery; but never before in life – only in dreams. And had he not awakened heart-broken, because he had failed to seize and question some vision of the night? Oh, stupidity, oh slowness, oh dull, heavy brain and lips of clay! He must speak to her – but what? There was nothing adequate – nothing that would preserve, instead of shattering, magic. Even his male voice, light though it was, seemed to him suddenly too harsh an instrument.

He jerked his head round so suddenly, looking for some retreat to which he could lead her when the hateful record had whirred out its last long-drawn chord, that Theresa looked up at him in mild surprise. She smiled; and at the side of her pointed chin, there appeared, absurdly and deliciously, a dimple. And Sylens laughed, a soft chuckle like a little boy's. He was astonished at the sound: he had not thought he could ever laugh like that again, with pure delight. Suddenly he was aware that the music had really stopped; and that Claribel and Gilbert were close beside them, revolving in a last slow turn. As Claribel's blonde head appeared from behind the barrier of Gilbert's dark shoulder, Sylens was conscious of her black eyes, expressionless and lightless and yet somehow baleful like a snake's or a lizard's, noticing him, registering... and worse still, reminding... reminding him of that day, or night, when first she had collected him, when with one of his poems dangling from her hand, she had laid her other hand on his hair, and drawn out of him the ultimate tribute – lying, yet he had uttered it; nothing, nothing, nothing to her, yet everything to him, who had never used that word before of any human being. 'You are the most *beautiful* thing I have ever seen': to her the most banal of compliments, to him a sacrilege, a blasphemy, a horrible misuse of words, when all he meant was that she had whipped his senses to fury – given him a salted draught and refused to slake his thirst, cheated and deceived him through his vanity, and his even more innocent longing to communicate, through poetry, what seemed to him so wonderful in the world. Poetry! She did not know the meaning of the word. She did not, nowadays, even bother to cut the pages of the books he gave her.

He turned to Theresa.

'Could we talk?' he said.

Theresa inclined her head, and laid her hand in the crook of his arm. He led her away from her sisters, to the opposite corner of the room.

## 5

John Carraway had been dancing with Ursula. They had talked all the time. When the dance was over he led her back to the place she had vacated, and sat down beside her, in Theresa's place.

'But tell me,' he said, 'what do you *not* do? You paint, you write verses, you read the classics, you embroider and have technical knowledge of a number of things. I suspect you of being able to mend electric bells or an aeroplane. You may be, for all I know, a doctor or a lawyer. How many languages have you? A dozen, or more?'

Ursula laughed. 'Languages – oh, that has been easy. We have lived in so many foreign towns.'

'Latvian? Magyar? Erse?'

Ursula laughed again. 'Not Erse – and oh, so very little Latvian.'

'No, but seriously,' said Carraway, 'what is your real life-work? Don't tell me that anyone has room, really, for more than one, to which everything else contributes. Either that or they have none at all. But it is inconceivable that you have none. You have one, and it is a large, vast, satisfying one – and for it you would do murder. Tell me – I won't give you away.'

'First tell me yours,' said Ursula, 'and then I shall know whether you are to be trusted.' He noticed, then, that she had the slightest trace of an un-English accent. It was not in the pronunciation, but in the choice and arrangement of words, and the value she gave to each of them. But then, she had been born in Moscow.

'I am,' he said quite seriously, 'a painter of trees.' His kindly, pleasant grey eyes grew soft and happy at the thought. 'Trees are living entities. They know the struggle for existence; they strive, not merely for self-preservation, but to fulfil some perfect form. Each one has its character and its history. In their shapes, their conformation to the ideal, their deviation from it, their distortions, one may read their victories and their defeats by environment. Their tragedy is, they cannot escape, they cannot move…' His eyes shone with interest in what he was saying, he ran a bony, strong hand through his tow-coloured hair. 'I will show you – you must come and see my sketches some time. You would be interested – but,' he suddenly recollected himself, 'this is all by the way. I have told you far more than you asked for. So you can't refuse to answer my question: What is your own life-work? I am sure it must be something much grander and of wider scope than mine.'

Ursula said: 'My life-work is – my sisters.'

Carraway gazed back at her, almost open-mouthed. She, too, was beautiful, with her fine glowing intelligent brown eyes and delicate nose and wide smile, though not so formally beautiful as Theresa.

'Is that so?' he said, and was silent for a minute or two, trying to express to himself her answer in terms of his own work. 'Do you mean,' he said at last, 'that you, as the eldest, regard it as your life-work to mould them, guide them, see that they are happy and a success in life? You wish,' he said, as light slowly dawned on him, 'to be always adequate to their needs, in little things and big? Is that why you *do* so many things – so that if, for instance, Theresa killed a man, or Lucy scalded her finger, you could equally easily protect the one, and heal the other?'

'You express it very well,' said Ursula, almost indulgently. She was not taking this conversation very seriously, Carraway saw, but all the same, her answer was true – and how very interesting. Her rich voice contained no hint of displeasure: he was free to weave theories about an obvious fact if he pleased.

'But that was the past,' Carraway went on eagerly. 'What about the future? They have been under your care till now; but this can't last, can it? I mean, Lucy is a woman, twenty-one or two, I suppose. And Theresa – People will fall in love with them, will want – no doubt have wanted – to marry them... By the way,' he said, suddenly turning on her, 'why haven't *you* married? *Are* you married?' He saw that the answer was 'no', and he felt pleased, for Ursula had that poise, that assurance and maturity, which is often associated with marriage, though she was clearly not more than about twenty-eight years of age. 'You are not married. Well. And no doubt that's part of your plan, for clearly it must be a matter of choice.'

He was not paying her an idle compliment; he was stating a fact, and if the fact had been contrary, he would have said it just as simply, for imperceptibly he had accepted her as someone to be spoken to as frankly as one would talk to oneself in one's own mind. This did not mean that he had forgotten that she was a woman. Carraway held the view that if it was right to hang men, or beat them or shoot them down on the field of battle or blow them to fragments by bombs dropped from above, all these treatments were equally right if inflicted on women. He wished that such a theory could be for a while put into practice, believing that this might bring the world to its senses about the game of murder that it called war. He believed that the collective reason of mankind is too embryonic to be appealed to yet, at this stage of evolution; but that one can sometimes achieve the desired result through their sentimentality. He had got himself into hot water more than once, by airing these views from soapboxes and in revolutionary periodicals... He divided the world into 'great guys' and 'sub-norms', and that served all his needs in categorizing human beings. The 'great guys' were people to whom one could talk; into the other category went, pell-mell, everybody of any age and either sex who was 'a mass of reflexes', or 'a mass of convention', or any other agglomeration which made communication impossible. Perhaps it was because 'great guys' were so rare that Carraway spent so much of his time with trees; for he was not one who enjoys having to dislike his fellows.

'That is to say,' he went on, 'if you have not married, it is for the sake of your sisters. Unless, of course, you haven't yet come into collision with anyone who will *do*.'

'Most men will do,' Ursula murmured, 'to give one children.'

'And that is what you would chiefly demand of marriage?'

'Yes.'

'Not companionship?'

'Not necessarily. That would be a piece of just too extraordinary good fortune, wouldn't it, if the father of one's children turned out to be anything more than a tolerable member of the household?'

'Or if he found the mother of his children more than a trustworthy business partner?'

'Exactly,' said Ursula.

'I don't disagree with you,' said Carraway, 'but I think you must have very high standards. Aren't they, really, fantastic? I use the word in its true meaning: conceived from your imagination, not derived from experience, nor brought within the compass of reality?'

'You are quite mistaken,' said Ursula, 'my standards are not in the least fantastic; they are based on immediate experience, the nearest and in fact the only experience I have.'

Carraway thought; and his mind quickly flashed back the answer. 'Your sisters?'

'Yes, my sisters.' She spoke the word softly, with great tenderness.

'Then your not marrying,' he persisted, 'is not related to your plan for them – not, that is, a self-denial on your part – but is simply due to lack of a candidate of pass-standard: there were no entries of sufficient merit, and so –'

'Oh no, no,' said Ursula laughing. 'You have not understood me. My standard for a *husband*, you remember, was the lowest possible...'

'But why *marry* the man merely to have a child?'

'Oh,' said Ursula, 'a hundred reasons. I am, you see, a complete realist. And at the present time, and in the society in which I live, one must marry the father of one's children, if one is not to cause embarrassment and discomfort to others.'

'Your sisters?' said Carraway mockingly.

'My sisters,' repeated Ursula again. 'Try as they would, you know, they could not really like it if I had an illegitimate child. For it would mean that others would think and speak harshly of me, and they would be distressed. Our harmony, our *inner* harmony, would be spoilt by discords coming from outside. They would accept my decision if I made it, and their very loyalty would bring pain to them, and suffering to me.'

'But if you married, they wouldn't mind?'

'Oh, not at all,' said Ursula. '*That* wouldn't make the slightest difference between us. But – I should prefer to see them come to fruition first, before I undertook the charge of a new family. I shall know at once if any such time ever arrives. But it has not come, yet. I am quite content to wait until, if ever, it does.'

'I see before me,' Carraway teased her, 'triple wedding: the three sisters. That will be an occasion! You will invite me? Not but that,' he added more seriously, 'I do feel a little sorry for your future husband. Poor fellow, he will be getting so much – and so little. He will think he is winning heaven, and all he will get will be' – he smiled, suddenly, sweetly, down at her – 'a tiny corner of it. You will admit him into the antechamber only; and then you will rattle the golden keys, an enormous bunch of them, under his nose. Is that fair? Is that kind? Is that –'

A dark shadow stood between them and the light. Carraway looked up: it was Gilbert, Claribel's husband. He was claiming Ursula for the next dance. Ursula rose, but Carraway stayed where he was. A golden rocket had suddenly soared up in his brain, a decision, a determination, a mad determination, to marry Ursula; mad because he would fall in love with her and do all she asked, fall in with her way of life, sacrifice his own. He would wait, if need be, for that triple wedding. And then he would give her the children she desired, to be his own successful rivals. He would do much better to run away, back to his beloved, silent, unexacting, ever-accommodating trees... Ha, ha, he did not care. Away with the bonnet, over the windmill! But what was there at the back of his mind, what voice, not of caution but of warning, telling him to remember? Why not face the truth, and admit that, when Gilbert's dark shadow had fallen across them, the golden rocket had come down, a spent and impotent stick, to ground?

He knew whose emissary Gilbert was. He had not needed to look up, to be aware of Claribel's baby smile, self-satisfied and inexorable, following the proceedings from the opposite side of the room...

Suddenly, the little round muscle at the corner of his jaw contracted; his fine mouth set itself in thin, unpleasant line, and his grey eyes narrowed till only a sinister glint in them was visible. As Ursula passed him in the dance, she gave him a charming smile; her gloves dangling from the hand that lay on Gilbert's forearm, brushed Carraway's hair. He lifted his eyes to hers, and there was despair in them.

Claribel, as she passed, let her fingers lightly brush his hair, where Ursula's glove had fallen. He shrank back; and his face, usually so kindly and humorous, almost whimsical, had become a mask, lined, pointed, evil. Claribel shrugged her shoulders: it was a long time since she had been able to bother with Carraway. He had not succeeded in wiping off from her pink round face that baby smile.

# 6

Markakis was enjoying himself. He grinned as he sorted the records, looking for fox-trots each noisier than the last, with more vulgar refrains. His black hair hung in a dark lock on his forehead: he ground his teeth as he turned – but carefully – the handle of the gramophone. It was no part of his desire to break the instrument: that would spoil the fun – *his* fun. He had to exercise great care, great restraint, not to give the handle that extra turn… He was, by now, well primed with champagne. Gilbert had carried round a tray of glasses; but the dancers, when the music started, were apt to come and leave their drink half-finished on the stone ledge above the fireplace. Some of them forgot to come back and reclaim them. Markakis, cunning and alert, counted them as his, and swilled them down. He was happy, now: his brain was aflame, with thoughts of Crete where he had been born; twenty-five years ago, after the accursed foreigners had come in their search for knowledge, to the cradle of civilization. His mother had been a peasant woman from Heracleon; his father an English gentleman dabbling in archaeology. He had taken his mother's name.

But his father had had money; and Markakis had taken money, since this was all he could get out of him. He did not even know his father's name. At seven years of age, Markakis had been fetched by strange men away from his mother and his grandfather and the vineyard and the one-storied hut in the fields above Knossos, where the English gentlemen – and ladies also – worked at their books, and sorted all the rubbish they collected among the ruins, joining together the bits of clay and putting the results in glass cases in the new museum in the town...

Then he had become an English schoolboy. No expense had been spared on his education. His holidays had been carefully planned, with tutors in England or abroad. When his musical talent became unmistakable that too had been fostered and catered for: there had been more journeys, with different solemn young men, to Vienna, Berlin, Paris, Warsaw... Oh those long train journeys across Europe, in first-class *wagons-lits*, the bored young man in one corner, the dark, sulky-looking Greek-English boy in the other. Few words were exchanged. Markakis despised these young university men who were paid to be his guardians: *paedagogoi*! Bah, in ancient Hellas, such people had been slaves. It amused Markakis to think how, in those days, if he, Markakis, had committed a murder, Smith or Jones or Fitzpatrick could, and probably would, have been handed over to the torture to have the evidence extracted from them...

Often, as the Mitropa ran sweetly across the plains, or among the pine-clad slopes, or beside the great wide rivers, Markakis would cease to register the scene passing before his eyes, and he would see instead the blue, smooth waters of the Bay of Candia, the snowy peak of Ida, the green winding valley leading south to Phaestos, the great Venetian aqueduct crossing the ravine near Knossos, the mules crossing a shallow stream, the meadows pink with wild gladioli in spring... He thought, too, of his grandfather, a man of great honour, a Phylax to one of the places where the English had been digging: a tall man with fierce moustaches, and a hollow in each cheek where a bullet had passed through, when he was fighting for Hellas in one of his many battles. Grandfather wore high boots, and black breeches with a great bag hanging down at the back, in which to carry provisions: he wore a blue jacket with black braid, and on Easter Day he sang in the church in a high nasal sing-song voice. The children were always hanging round him and on to him; even when he talked to the important visitors who came to see the excavations, the children wouldn't leave him alone; they would cling with their arms round his boot-legs, and climb, swinging on the folds of his breeches. He would bear it all for a long time without noticing, as if a fly had settled on his nose – and then, suddenly, he would shout in a great, fierce, rough voice, and his long moustache would bristle. The children would flee, like minnows in a pool when one drops a stone; but they knew it meant nothing, and in a few seconds they were all back again. Grandfather had never been known to strike anyone, except for the glory of Hellas; and he used to carry the luggage for the English girl-students, if he liked them, down to the quay, for nothing but love. His moustache bristled so fiercely if they tried to protest, that they always gave way...

Ah, Crete, jewel of the Mediterranean! And to think that once he had thought Claribel a symbolic embodiment of all that Crete had been, and had likened her, in his music, to Ariadne, to the Snake-Goddess, to the lovely girls of the ancient bull-ring, with their slim waists and long slender legs, that he had seen on the palace frescoes of his home! Just because, when he had shown her, reverently, first the drawings of those wonderful works of art, the source of the inspiration of Hellas, and then translated them for her into music, and she had agreed with his enthusiasm – reflected it, from the blank smooth surface that was her soul! Claribel, a Minoan princess! Bah, they would have thrown her to the Minotaur!

With trembling, nervous hands he slid out a horrible rumba from the pile, and set it turning... Tick, tick-tick, tick, tock – so many nails into the skull of Claribel, devourer of souls… His eyes slewed round to the stone ledge: two more half-emptied glasses of champagne, and a thimble of Benedictine…

## 7

The two makeweights had not been asked to dance this one. They were called Betty and Peggy: Betty was tall and slim and fair, and Claribel at the moment maintained that she was beautiful, but no one would agree with Claribel, because to the others a straight nose, eyes and mouth in the right place, a good forehead and wavy hair – all the ingredients of beauty, that is to say – were not enough, and they demanded that unifying something which Betty did not possess. They did agree, however, that it was astonishing how she failed to be beautiful, since she had the necessary features aided by the bloom of seventeen. One had to be careful how one put this to Claribel, for Claribel was making a sketch of her, and was apt to confuse her own version with the original… 'Perhaps,' Carraway had said slyly, pouring oil on troubled waters. 'Betty will *grow* to be beautiful, when she has your portrait of her to go upon.' This had appeased Claribel.

Peggy had no pretensions to beauty: she was round and soft and roguish-looking, with curly short hair and soft moist lips and twinkling eye. She got on, as a rule, very well with men: but she was soon aware that she was not going to score her usual easy success here. This was puzzling: Gilbert had danced with her, and said not a word, but then, of course, everyone knew how boringly devoted he was to Claribel; he was a polite host, and waited each time until the other men had made their choice of partners; then he chose a wallflower. It was no compliment to be danced with by

Gilbert. And he was so thin and morose, one was afraid to address him for fear of saying something silly; anything would sound silly, said to him. He was so tall that one could not even catch his eye; he stared intently, his chin well above the top of one's topmost curls, into the distance as he skilfully steered one round the room. Peggy had her eye on a gay-looking young man with golden curls who had just come in, and who, she heard, was an actor; but at present he was absorbed in a low, laughing conversation with Claribel. However, there was plenty of time. Her stout, short little feet itched to dance, so much so that she would have liked to seize thin Betty and whisk her round, in default of a male partner. But she had sufficient *savoir faire* to realize that such girlish antics would be quite out of place here, among all these snobs and highbrows... She felt a little resentful towards Claribel, who had asked her here and promised her a good time, with lots of amusing men; Claribel herself had always seemed so simple and natural and not stuck-up, at the art school: a girl among girls, yet wise and understanding as older women should be and too often are not. Her advice was always to go ahead and take what you can get, while the going's good...

Yes, Peggy and Betty were having a thin time so far. Here they were, sitting side by side on the fender-seat: Betty was pretending she didn't care to dance because her shoes hurt her, and was making a futile attempt, which nobody heeded, to give the excuse verisimilitude by poking her finger between shoe and foot, and looking pained. Peggy was pretending nothing; if she was to be out of things, she meant to look it, and then somebody would have to take notice and do something. She knew – being shrewder than Betty – how ready people are to accept one's false excuses when it suits them to do so. Pride is a luxury for which one pays dear.

Betty and Peggy did not know each other. But here they were, squashed together on the same fender-seat, and so they were obliged to fraternize.

'You given up dancing?' said Peggy in a friendly tone not without a flavour of malice.

'Yes,' drawled Betty with a defensive frown. The finger-poking and foot-rubbing was renewed with greater energy.

'My shoes hurt me – here – and – and here –'

Peggy didn't bother to look convinced. 'You know Claribel well?' she said inquisitively.

Betty tossed her head. 'She is going to do my portrait.'

'In oils?'

'I don't know. She is sketching me, and waiting for the right medium to – er – *evince* itself.'

Peggy recognized a Claribel word. 'You paying?'

'My father is.'

'Much?'

'I don't think it's been settled yet. It was Claribel's idea. She said I had such perfect features, she wanted to do a mask of them. But of course, we couldn't let her do it for nothing.'

'Well, my advice is,' said Peggy, 'settle it quickly and get your Papa to write a cheque for it, and then she'll do you in marble. Otherwise it may be concrete, you know.'

Betty tossed her head again. 'Has she done a portrait of *you*?' she inquired with an edge on her voice.

'Oh, hundreds,' said Peggy cheerfully. 'She uses me in the nude to practise on. *I* am supposed to have a marvellous figure. I'd show you, but one can't do a thing here.'

'Oh, she employs you,' said Betty. She tried saying this in a neutral, disinterested voice, for she did not want to offend the plump little girl just yet, when goodness knew how long she might now have to sit beside her. Also, Peggy looked like one who would not be content to wait for ever; and she might, if they were allies, drag Betty in after her. Perhaps she ought to have chosen some other word...

Peggy did not appear to find the word at all offensive.

'Employ my eye,' she said, 'if you mean does she *pay* me. Not a bit of it. She *uses* me. It is supposed to be a favour, merely to be in her studio and watch her at work and pick up tips. And I can assure you,' her voice sank to a low gurgle, and she approached her curly head to Betty's, 'it's worth my while, or I wouldn't do it. One gets tips about more things than drawing and modelling...' Her eyes twinkled unspeakable mysteries.

'What do you mean?' Betty's thin, well-modelled nose drew near to Peggy's *retroussé* one; she was shocked, scandalized and intently eager. 'What does she tell you?'

'Oh, all the things a girl wants to know – about men, and all that –'

'Men.' Betty breathed the word with an almost religious awe and fervour. But she remembered that she was her father's dear, good little girl, pure as a snowdrop; and also that she was a lady, whereas Peggy was a vulgar little art student from goodness knew where. So she suppressed the questions burning on her lips, and said instead, glancing casually round the room:

'Who *are* all these people? Do you know them?'

'Oh, by repute. They're all more or less famous.'

'Yes?' Now they were on safe ground, and Betty could display her eagerness. She preened herself, and sat upright, as her sense of failure fell from her, for she was a doctor's daughter, and no famous people ever came to her home. Her mother would brag to the neighbours: 'Only think, Betty was at a party last night, the celebrated Mrs Lorimer's you know, the sculptress' – Betty's mother could not be cured of referring to women artists as 'poetess', 'authoress' and so on – 'and there was such a distinguished gathering. There was So-and-so the painter, and So-and-so –'

'Tell me their names,' she said; 'I didn't quite get them all when they were introduced. Such a crowd!' She laughed artificially. She now perceived that she had underestimated Peggy, who was obviously in the swim, and that she must hasten to make up for lost time and secure her friendship, for this evening anyway.

'Well, that's John Carraway, the painter,' began Peggy accommodatingly, 'he's a dear, but quite hopeless because he has trees on the brain and you can be introduced to him fifty times and he'll never know you. He'll cut you dead, though he has the sweetest nature and wouldn't hurt a daisy in a meadow. And that dark man talking to the new girl over there in the corner is the poet, Paul Sylens; he's awfully learned though he looks so young; I had a *grande passion* for him once, in the distance, but I realized he was not for the likes of me. He comes to Claribel's studio sometimes, and they talk the most awful rot about Strophe and Antistrophe in Life and Art, and he quotes chunks of Greek at her and she's bored stiff really, but she keeps her end up quite well, considering. Then the lad at the gramophone is Markakis, the composer; and that grim-looking man talking to the stout boy is a miniature artist, and the fat boy paints battle-scenes ten feet square. The curly-headed one talking to Claribel is an actor – I don't know his name, but I mean to find out quite soon –' She was beginning to get tired of priming Betty, and her information dwindled off to a thinner and thinner trickle.

'Who are the three girls who came in last?' Betty persisted, noticing Peggy's wandering eye, and determined not to be put off until she had got all she wanted.

'I don't know.' Peggy was bored. 'Except that they don't belong here. They look expensive and dilettante so I suppose they're clients of Claribel's. They seem quite unaware of the sort of show they've stepped into. I wonder that Claribel risked it.'

'Risked what?'

'Well, surely you know what is the great bond uniting all the distinguished company – except you and me, of course, and we're disqualified by sex.'

'What?' cried Betty, raising her voice in her excitement and irritation.

Peggy looked back at her with amused contempt. 'Why, they're all Claribel's lovers, of course. Have been, or will be – for I see a few new faces here. And what's more, they all know it – know about the others, I mean. That's Claribel's genius. She's got masks of them all over her walls – scalps if you like…'

'Her lovers!' Betty quite forgot to control her voice in her horror and ecstasy. 'But her *husband* – isn't she *afraid* –'

Peggy chuckled flatly. 'Gilbert? Oh, he doesn't count except as the Grand Master of the Ceremonies. He spends his time playing up to her and keeping her happy, because he's afraid she'll divorce him. She has been threatening to for years, so they say, and he believes her. Perhaps he's right; at any rate, there's one man here she might do it for, if she ever did it for anybody. At least, I thought he was here, but he seems to have vanished. Perhaps he hasn't come downstairs. He's her *real* husband, so they say. Gilbert is her lackey, and the others are just *objets d'art*, pieces she's collected in her off moments. But he's the one who really owns her. *He's* not an artist or a writer; he's a sailor, an explorer, and things of that kind, though he has more brains than the whole crowd of us put together, one's told. Didn't you see him upstairs? An immensely tall, broad, raw-faced man, with hair going thin on top; a great head like a lion's or a sphinx's, and –'

A large hand was stretched out from behind, and came to rest, very lightly, on Peggy's shoulder, between the two girls. A voice, pleasant, slow, not loud but very clear and vibrant, said:

'Here I am, Peggy. Tell your friend to look at me; that will save you the trouble of further description.'

Peggy's mouth dropped open; but no more words came. Betty, blushing all over, concentrated her gaze on her thin hands clenched tightly in her lap. Neither of the girls looked round. When two of the young men came at last to claim them for the next dance, they both sprang to their feet and flung themselves into the welcome and welcoming arms, and allowed themselves, without a backward glance, to be swept away.

## 8

Marcus Praed leaned back again on the oak settle beside Lucy; his large body filled the rest of it, so that there was no longer room for anyone else to sit down beside them. He was not wearing evening dress, but a rough tweed suit, and a soft low collar; he looked, therefore, like an inmate of the house who had drifted in accidentally, not knowing there was a party. Apparently he did not mean to dance; for he wore thick brown shoes, well creased across the toes. All he needed was a knobbed stick to equip him completely for walking.

'She chose her adjectives very badly, I thought,' he said calmly to Lucy. 'Tall, broad, raw-faced, with hair going thin – and yet I cannot deny that each one of them is true. I wonder how it is that words, used accurately one by one, never succeed in conveying the right visual impression. That little girl has a clear image of my physical appearance on her mind: and she has words, plenty of them. Yet she cannot put them together. It reminds me of an experience I had when a child: I suddenly decided to learn French, and one day my mother came upon me looking up words in the French dictionary. I was " translating", according to my lights, a story from English into French in this way, word by word… It was a shock to me when she explained that one did not turn English into French by such a simple process. I realized that life was much more difficult than I had thought… I often ask myself,' he said, looking round the room, 'what *is* composition?

Now surely here is a gathering of people that ought to be able to enlighten me.'

His gaze went calmly round, from one to another of the company. Lucy was moved to admire his coolness: one would not have guessed that he was thus looking over the assemblage of the lovers, past, present and future, of his own mistress, his unofficial 'wife'; one could not even tell if the gossip he overheard was news to him or not. She weighed both alternatives, and was unable to decide. How easily, with what masterly skill, he had led her far away from the personal theme to a topic of extreme abstractness! She decided that she would like to know him better, if it were possible ever to know such a man at all. He seemed the soul of serene sincerity – and was not this the mark of the arch-dissimulator? Self-control like his could carry off anything, even murder, without betraying a sign. She wondered, irrelevantly, if he ever had killed anyone. Those large hands...

'You must be wondering,' he went on in the same impersonal tone, 'what truth there was in the little girl's story. That is, unless you have a positively inhuman lack of curiosity – and I shouldn't think you are inhuman in *any*thing.' He surveyed her, a little from above and behind, for she was leaning forward, her profile outlined against the fire. She had Theresa's delicate straight nose, and Ursula's full lips and rich dark hair; and at first one might have thought her a compromise between them, and therefore less interesting, as she was less conspicuous; she was even physically smaller than either, her younger sister having already outstripped her in height. But her high clear brow was her own, and also the slight widening out of her nostrils, and the tilt of her mouth on one side as she talked. And gradually one became aware of the mainspring of her character, which was courage, unending courage. Her small hand and delicate wrist caught Marcus's eye, and he thought of what he had noticed many times in his life of adventure and danger, how will and spirit, housed in a delicate frame, can achieve results undreamt of by those who worship physical power. He was himself of surpassing physical strength, and rejoiced in this gift; but to be excessively admired for that was not to his liking.

She answered him frankly. 'No, strangely enough, it hadn't occurred to me. I think, if you hadn't reminded me, it wouldn't have occurred to me, at any rate until I was no longer in your presence.' She thought. 'Yes – and it was your doing: you led me so quickly and cleverly away.'

'Shall I tell you?' he said temptingly.

'If you like. But I warn you, I am not curious. Enough for me that it's no business of mine.'

'I believe you,' he said. 'How lucky you are! And how still more lucky the people you live with!'

'Why?' Lucy's glance shot quickly down the room, to where Theresa and Ursula were now sitting together, with Carraway and Sylens beside them.

'Because if you are not curious, then you also lack that most noxious of the minor vices, the passion to interfere in other people's lives.'

Lucy shook her head. 'You're wrong. I have the desire to interfere, so strongly developed that I have never dared to look too closely. I prefer, in self-defence, to shut my eyes.'

'Ah, that's where you love deeply. And your loves are deep, but not wide.'

'I love *every*body,' said Lucy stubbornly. 'But I do not wish to alter them, that's all.'

'Then you don't know the meaning of jealousy, either? You can't conceive of wanting to kill someone rather than let him or her interfere with what you regard as yours?'

'I regard nothing as mine,' said Lucy sombrely. 'I never have, and never shall.'

'Not even on the strength of a solemn vow, such as marriage?'

'No one has the power to give away the future,' said Lucy. 'It is not ours to bestow.'

'Then you never make a vow?'

'No.'

'Because,' he leaned towards her, 'if you did, not Satan and all his angels could prevent you from keeping it?'

'Perhaps.'

'Then may I never come within the range of a *hatred* such as yours would be.'

For the first time Lucy turned on him the direct scrutiny of her dark, unwavering eyes. 'Why do you say that? You make it sound like a challenge. I assure you, you are wasting your ingenuity. I am, as you see me, completely commonplace, in my likings and dislikings. I love people, that is all. I don't wish to possess and bind. I wish to be, and leave others, free – free to be themselves, and so more interesting than anything I could make of them. As for hatred: I hate only one thing, and that is to see anyone trying to take away freedom from a soul intended by nature to be free. The only motive that could make me kill would be, I think, the desire to rid the world of a tyrant, a usurper of souls.' There was a throb of passion in her voice, and this did not escape Marcus. He said casually:

'Then I gather you don't sympathize with me in my present quandary?'

Lucy waited. If she was startled she gave no sign.

'You heard,' he went on suavely, 'little Peggy's account of the situation in which we all find ourselves. Take away her melodramatic interpretation, and the facts which remain are correct.'

Lucy's bright eyes watched him unblinkingly.

'By a compact which must seem strange to you, who don't know its history, it was understood that, in the life of Claribel, Gilbert relinquished his position to me. Virtually, that is, of course: we did not wish to call on the law to rearrange our affairs for us. His position is a hard one, I'm afraid; whether he finds it so or not, I don't know, and am too much of an egoist to care. It was sufficient for me that he preferred it to the only other alternative, which was to lose Claribel entirely. He has not complained; and he has fulfilled his side of the bargain with faultless honour, for he is a gentleman, and being a gentleman can lead one into strange courses of action sometimes...' He laid his two hands, one above the other, upon his knee-cap. He might, as he gazed blandly round the room, his head inclined conversationally towards Lucy, have been telling her the story of his latest discoveries in Mexico.

'Now I am an explorer,' he said, 'among other things, and that entails being a great deal away from home. I explained to Claribel that I expected her to wait for me. I did not expect miracles of self-denial on her part. She is an attractive woman, and a perfectly normal one. But – and she knew this when the arrangement was made, as long as twelve years ago – there were things I would not tolerate. That is to say, I was not a second Gilbert, not one of a series, but the chief, the essential factor in her being, or nothing. I demanded, and I gave, an intimacy which should be too close for lying – too real for trivial adventurers on either side to affect it. There was only one thing indispensable, and that was truth.'

Lucy was listening now, intently, almost like a small girl. He did not trouble to glance down at her, as he pursued his story.

'So that you see how what I have just heard was a somewhat disagreeable shock to me. If I had been on the spot, such self-deception would have been impossible... As it is, I must admit to having relied too much on the spoken, and written, word… My dignity is offended, my pride brought low, my confidence in my own judgement and the power of my personality to maintain its hold even in absence, annihilated.' He laughed quietly.

'What will you do about it?' said Lucy, her chin on her hands.

He shrugged his shoulders. 'What is there to do? I could make a scene, curse Gilbert, even beat Claribel, but what would be the use? She is as she is. The fault was mine. My mistake, my stupidity. Do you know,' he turned to her almost eagerly, 'I think it may have arisen from my never-to-be-exaggerated egoism. You see, I had a *theory* about love.'

Lucy raised her fine brows as if this were the most extraordinary thing he had yet confided to her. Claribel, looking at them, thought they were getting on nicely, and smiled to think how much dear Marcus, with his love of telling anecdotes, and making intellectual conquests, must be enjoying himself.

'When I first met Claribel,' pursued Marcus serenely, 'I had had no serious love-affairs. Nothing had ever seriously touched me. I had my own concerns, sport, friendships, hobbies and all that; for me, women didn't exist. I thought love, as a sentiment, a soft and silly thing, and I pitied those who suffered from it, or appeared to – for I didn't quite believe in it; one doesn't quite believe in things one hasn't oneself experienced… At eighteen I joined an exploration party going to Greenland. I used to watch with a sort of pitying curiosity other men of the party writing home letters to their girls or their wives. I saw what the mails meant to them when they did come, usually after delays. I saw how they suffered when there was a scare lest the boat that was coming to fetch us away shouldn't arrive before the ice closed, which would mean a whole long winter more away from home. The boat came in time by about twelve hours only. I saw them go to pieces with joy – I saw men who had stood unbelievable hardships *weep* with relief. And I was puzzled. I felt my own indifferent state *must* be better; but I wasn't quite sure... It was on my return from this expedition that I first met Claribel.'

He sank into silence.

Lucy waited. At last she said tentatively, 'You said you had a *theory?*'

Marcus roused himself. 'Oh yes,' he said, 'the theory. Well, I met Claribel. And, to cut a long story short, I decided I would use her – I would find out. I would agree to devote myself, to give up my will and let myself be influenced by another person, and see what this led to. I decided to allow myself to fall in love. Of course, I did in those days believe Claribel to be – something much greater than she is, or claims to be. One must allow that even at her silliest, she is more interesting than many cleverer people, because she is never the same. The fact is – but I didn't know this then – that there is no such person as Claribel. She is a mirror – and her variety is that of the countless people who pass before her and are temporarily reflected...'

'I see,' said Lucy. 'So that is why you are so calm. You were never in love with her at all.'

'Is that how it strikes you?' said Marcus, interested. 'But don't be misled by my appearance of indifference. What I felt may not have been love as *you* mean it – and,' he turned to her so suddenly that she flinched slightly, though she would not withdraw, 'I am sure it was not. I am sure, now, I have never been in love, yet... But that doesn't alter Claribel's side of it. She has pretended to be mine. She has professed to satisfy my colossal egoism. And she has cheated, thus wasting my time. Twelve years is a very long time to keep a man in a state of blindness, so that he can't go on to further discoveries. How do I know what I've missed? How do I know what she has robbed me of? It's not the loss of *her* that counts – that's nothing, she is worthless, and for years I've found her silly and boring, with an infantile mind – it's the loss of the opportunities she has prevented my finding and taking. And that's all over. But I bear her a grudge, a deep grudge for it, all the same...'

'Would you do her harm, if you could?'

'Yes, if it weren't too much trouble,' said Marcus calmly. 'But it almost certainly will be. After I leave this house to-night, I shall never see her again, except by unavoidable accident.'

'But you can see your whole life change from the bottom upwards, so suddenly, and speak of it – to a stranger, without a qualm?'

'Oh,' said Marcus, 'I was given that gift – of ready adaptation – from birth. Already to me Claribel is a distant speck on the horizon, a port I have left for ever, or a ship in which I shall never sail again...' He stood up. 'Shall we dance?' He seemed unaware of his rough suit and clumsy shoes.

Lucy made no demur. He held her, not closely and strongly as she had expected and half-feared, but rather loosely, and he danced without much enthusiasm, as if absent-mindedly. But on his face, that Peggy had described as 'raw', there was a look of calm determination, of a purposiveness so strong that it took Lucy's breath.

## 9

Claribel clapped her hands.

'Now listen, everybody,' she said. 'I think it's time we had a change from dancing. Let's play a game.'

All looked expectantly towards her. There were some who had just begun to enjoy the dancing, and were sorry to have to stop – but that is how things usually happen: at first one is indifferent, then one's interest is captured, and one lets oneself be drawn on, till one is completely off one's guard. And then one may be sure there will be an interruption. However, nobody would have dreamt of protesting; all were much too polite to voice any criticism of the arrangements of their hostess, whose baby voice expressed nothing except desire for their enjoyment. Also, they thought, probably she would prove correct in the long run; for no one could deny that Claribel, whatever else she did or didn't do, had a genius for providing pleasure. Part of this genius lay in her knowing when to cause other people to stop.

The guests had arranged themselves round the walls of the room. Partners had relinquished partners, to give their attention to Claribel. There had been a re-sorting: the three sisters, for instance, had found time to slip quietly back into their places, together on the oak settle. They, too, looked towards Claribel with courteous interest.

'Now what shall we play?' said Claribel. 'Oh well, I suppose we might as well begin right away with murder-party. Everyone likes that best. We have time for two or three draws before supper; and after supper we can have more dancing and more murder-party and any other games we can think of. Gilbert!'

Gilbert stood beside her with the pieces of paper already folded up on a tray. At her word he stepped forward, and began his round of the room.

The three sisters consulted together, Ursula and Theresa leaning forward round Lucy until their foreheads almost touched.

'Will someone kindly explain to us,' said Ursula emerging, 'how the game is played?'

'What!' cried all the old friends. 'You don't know how to play murder-party? Oh, you are lucky! You will get a thrill.' Several pressed forward to explain; but the great bulk of Marcus barred the way for the rest. He said in his clear, pleasant voice:

'We each take a piece of paper from Gilbert's tray. Most of the papers are blank. But one has the word Murderer written on it, and another the word Detective. Whoever draws the latter stays here, at the base. The others will withdraw, and wander about the house, which is in complete darkness. All know that one of their number is the murderer. We grope our way about. Presently one of us is murdered.'

'Dear me!' murmured Theresa: her sisters looked at her with affectionate smiles.

'That is to say,' went on Marcus deliberately, 'the murderer, having stalked his victim, indicates his deed by – what is the gesture, Claribel? Oh yes, of course – by placing his hands round the throat of the murderee.'

'Oh, hurry up, Marcus,' said Claribel pettishly. 'Tell them plainly. You use such long involved sentences. You are wasting time.'

Marcus went on imperturbably. 'The victim counts ten. The murderer has just so long in which to make good his or her escape.

Then the victim lets out a scream. At that sound, everybody stays where he happens to find himself. The lights go up. The detective comes, locates the body, notes the whereabouts of the rest of the party. Then we all come back here.'

'Oh,' said Lucy, 'is that all?'

Marcus shook his head. 'No, the main feature of the game is still to come: the detection. The detective questions us. We are bound to reply truthfully, all of us except the murderer, who may tell lies. If the criminal is not found within a given limit of time, the detective has to pay a forfeit.'

'I feel very nervous,' said Lucy. 'Do you think I could stay here this time?'

'You may be the detective, if you like,' said Marcus. 'I believe this is a privilege sometimes granted to tyros. Am I right, Claribel? I remember,' he said laughing, 'the time we first played murder-party at one of Claribel's parties, and Claribel herself was so nervous that she wouldn't leave the fire. So she had to be detective for the whole evening. But one soon gets over that and wants to be in the fun.'

Lucy said: 'I should like to be the detective this time.'

Marcus turned. 'Will whoever has drawn the detective's lot give it up to' – he realized he did not know her name – 'to this lady? Ah,' he said, turning back to her, 'and to think that before the New Year comes in, you will be fretting because you've drawn a blank again, instead of murderer!'

Markakis, from the shadow by the door, said sulkily, 'I'm the detective. Here you are.' He crossed the room, rather stiffly, to hand his paper to Lucy. Claribel snatched it from him.

'There's no need, idiot, to pass it on,' she said crossly. 'Gilbert will come round with the tray and collect them, for the next time, when you have all drawn.'

Gilbert had come, last of all, to the three sisters. Ursula and Theresa took their papers from the tray, looked at them, looked at each other, smiling, as if about to confer as was their habit; and then remembering that they mustn't tell, made solemn faces and dropped the papers on to Gilbert's tray again.

'Are we all ready?' cried Claribel. 'Come on, everybody!' The gathering began to move towards the door; Ursula and Theresa rose. By common consent a lane was made for them. The other girls followed, protesting that they didn't know the way, asking if one could go anywhere. The men closed in behind them.

'Claribel's house is perfect for this game,' said Marcus to Lucy as he prepared to follow. 'It is rambling and has many rooms, and odd twists and turns, which mislead one. One can easily take a wrong turning, and get quite lost – find oneself in somebody's bedroom when one thought one was still on the stairs.' He drifted off after the others.

Markakis, who had not been arrested by Claribel's gesture, made his way across the room, and took his place beside Lucy. Gilbert, the last to go through the door, noticed him.

'Aren't you playing, Markakis?' he said in the reproving tone he used towards all who ran counter to Claribel's arrangements.

'No,' snapped Markakis sullenly. 'I've given up my part, but I'm not going to be a blank, for anybody.' He huddled himself up in his corner.

Gilbert saw it was no use, and went away.

When they had all gone – when the door had closed behind Gilbert, and the room was still, Lucy turned to Markakis and said:

'I'm afraid you're cross because I stole your part.'

Markakis looked up from his brooding, and smiled. 'Oh, no,' he said. 'I just didn't want to play. I don't care for the game. I don't like games, and I like this one less than most.' He spoke quietly and reasonably, and if he was drunk, it was not obtrusive. 'And as you see, I don't dance. So really I can't think what I'm doing at the party.'

'But I heard you making lovely music upstairs,' said Lucy.

'Did you like it?' said Markakis eagerly. And then, remembering rebuffs, he said cautiously, glancing at her out of the sides of his eyes, 'I was playing Chopin. You liked that. Naturally, everybody does. Who could help it? But that doesn't make him any the less great.' He made his last statement defiantly, as if he expected it to be challenged.

'No, of course not,' said Lucy abstractedly. 'But you played other things that I didn't recognize. It was difficult to hear.'

'Did you like those?' He could not resist the question. Exaltation mounted up in him at the thought that here, once again, might be someone who understood the language of wordless sounds. This was so rare that one was happy to talk even to someone who had grasped the alphabet and the elementary syntactical rules. But knowledge, real knowledge, of the structure and the spirit – why, most people didn't know sense from gibberish, when it came to music.

'I was interested,' said Lucy thoughtfully. 'I should have liked to hear more.'

'You might well be,' said Markakis, 'for the theme of my last piece happened to be yourself – yourself and your two sisters, and the relationship between the three of you.'

'But you had scarcely seen us!' Lucy exclaimed.

'You had appeared for a minute. And the company began discussing you. They discussed who you were. I found myself playing out that theme, and the possible solutions of the mystery.'

Lucy was silent. He wondered if he had displeased her – if she thought he had taken too great a liberty. One could not tell. At any rate she made him feel that he must not say more. He crouched back resentfully into his corner. He wondered why, nowadays, everybody seemed able to have this effect on him. He had been self-confident enough once upon a time.

'Why didn't *you* want to play?' he said gruffly, at last. 'You weren't really nervous.'

'I am playing,' said Lucy calmly.

'Yes – but you insisted on being detective, though it wasn't your turn. That was a polite way of saying you didn't wish to join in the game. People don't play murder-party for the detection. It's the groping about in the dark they like, and –'

A loud bump, apparently just outside the door, startled them. Lucy stiffened and sat upright, and for a moment her face looked set and her eyes dark with alarm.

'Just somebody falling downstairs,' said Markakis. 'So you *are* nervous. Own up to it – there's nothing to be ashamed of. I'm just the same. To tell you the truth,' he said, leaning forward, 'I picked out the detective paper purposely. I was standing here while Gilbert was writing them, and I happened to see how each was folded. Would you like to be murderer next time? If so I'll tell you how to spot the paper. Murderer is the next best thing to be, if you are nervous, because then you are stalking the others and you know no one is stalking you.'

'So you have often played this game?'

'Often. Claribel's parties usually resolve themselves into it. You see, Claribel likes it above everything, because she's the one who usually gets murdered – if the murderer is a man.'

'And is that a great honour – to be murdered?'

'*Malista,*' nodded Markakis. As he watched Lucy, her small body, her head somewhat large for her size, her wide brow and dark hair, and the blue folds of her frock falling down to her red slippers, he was suddenly aware of a new clarity of vision, of inner vision – not about her, but about Claribel. He felt he could explain Claribel, down to the smallest cell in her body, the most minute reaction of her mind; there was not one of her motives he did not understand, not one of her purposes he could not perceive through the veils of false reasoning in which she shrouded it. The last piece of the puzzle fell into place. He, as an artist, was doomed and damned, and she had done it: she had undermined his confidence, and after first removing his greatest support, his friend the student-of-mathematics Leibbrandt, she had led him along a false trail of pseudo-psychology, to his present plight. Leibbrandt had gone back to Germany now, and never even wrote to him. What a loss was there! Why, helped by Leibbrandt, he had almost learnt to *talk* about music, in terms of another speech, that of mathematical proportion. Well, Claribel had not been able to seduce Leibbrandt. He had just laughed at her, and the 'rot' she talked; and he and Markakis had quarrelled. Now it was too late. He was done for...

But was he? A decadent Greek? No, a Cretan, an islander, the son of warriors, gentle as lambs, fierce as mountain boars. He looked at Lucy, and something whispered 'Courage!'

'What I shall dislike most,' she said mildly, 'is the scream.'

'Oh, that's nothing. You'll get used to that.'

'Never,' said Lucy in a low, fierce voice. 'You see, when I was a small child, about five, my father was – murdered. They took us to look on. Not my mother – she was too ill – Theresa was not yet born. But myself, and Ursula, and our nurse. They stood my father against a wall in the courtyard. Just as they were taking aim our nurse screamed. So they struck her down. Then they fired.'

'I see,' said Markakis, 'I see.' He put out his hands, and took hold of her two arms, under the elbows, so that she was forced to turn. He gazed for a long time into her face. 'Then I was right,' he said, 'and I *have* seen your face before, and your sisters'. All the world has, hundreds of times. If it were uttered, everybody here would know your name.'

Lucy nodded. 'But it will not be uttered.'

'No. Does Claribel know?'

'Yes. But it is a condition of our being here, that she does not tell. We are in London for a short visit only. When we have gone no one here will remember us. We thought,' she added wistfully, 'it would be nice to get away for once, and come to a real English party... Of course, we can leave at any moment. There are people waiting for us outside.'

'When I have written down what I played to-night I shall send it to you,' said Markakis. 'I know now what happened when you – the three of you – came into the room: at that moment I was – saved.'

The bumpings and slidings had continued. Suddenly the house was quiet, and a scream, sharp and raucous, rang out. Markakis was still holding Lucy by the elbows. She made no move, but her hands tightened on his forearms. They stayed like this for a while. Then Lucy gently withdrew.

'I think,' she said quietly, 'they too have had time to count ten by now,' and she rose and crossed the room.

Markakis ran before her, to open the door.

## II

The rest of this first game was quickly over, for nobody was much interested in the answer. Lucy had no great trouble in guessing it, within the stipulated time. And this was fortunate, for Claribel was showing some small signs of impatience, while the investigation proceeded. She was still smiling; but there were certain slight jerks of the head and blinkings of the eyes which those who knew her well recognized as danger signals. Lucy was unhurried: she asked each person one question, and then, for no apparent reason, fastened on Peggy as the murderer.

'But how did you guess?' cried Peggy gleefully, happy to have her secret displayed. 'I was miles away from him when you found me!'

'I examined the body,' said Lucy gravely. The golden-haired actor, whom everybody now knew as Desmond, smiled rather self-consciously; for it was he round whose neck Peggy's plump fingers had curled, and her pursuit and the liquid gaze of her round green eyes were, he feared, going to make him look silly before the evening was over. As if he weren't finding Mrs Lorimer quite enough to handle! Already he was conscious of having fallen short of her expectations. She had given him his clue, how to find her in the dark – and he had missed it. Purposely, because he had funked it – for one couldn't mistake the perfume she wore; and once she had even run her hands over his hair; but he had pretended not to be sure, and had slipped away among the other men. He hadn't known she would move so swiftly. And now, this schoolgirl! He was between two fires.

Lucy had scarcely had time to get out her reply when Claribel clapped her hands again.

'Another game!' she said. 'Who's ready for another game? Come on, Gilbert. Pass the lots round.'

The tray circulated. When it came to Lucy's end, Markakis, who was leaning in the corner behind her, murmured, 'It's still there.'

Lucy's hand hovered for a second; then passed over the piece he indicated, and chose another.

The party stumbled off into the dark again. Some of them started to grope their way downstairs, towards cellars and store rooms; others preferred the warmer, carpeted rooms upstairs. The whole house was thrown open, even the kitchens, for the servants had been sent off for the day, and would not reappear till morning. Doors were ajar, or yielded at a touch. Even if one tried to keep to the level, one found oneself descending a step here, ascending two steps there; one groped along an iron rail and found it ending in an ornamental twirl. From the nearby darkness came sounds of hard breathing; and farther away, sudden bumps, suppressed laughter, a rush of feet, groans. The guests were warming up to the game.

The three sisters, having given the others the slip, found themselves together in the kitchen. They had hidden in a recess just behind the door of the room they had left; and they had stayed there, while groping hands waved within inches of their faces, until the Indian file had passed them and been split into several parties by the stairs. If there had been a glimmer of light, Ursula's diamonds would have caught it; but when once the door closed, the darkness was complete. The sisters were aware of the groping hands because of the slight draught they created, and because one at least wore a luminous wrist-watch. Lucy was able to read the time: it said ten minutes to eight. When the sounds had all receded to a safe distance they emerged from their niche, and walked calmly and noiselessly down the corridor till they came to an end door. This was delightful: they need not take any further part in the game until someone screamed; then they would walk out again, dispose themselves separately on the stairs, and appear to have been wandering about all the time. The kitchen, besides being the least likely place where anyone else would come – for it was too direct and obvious – had also the advantage of being warm. The huge fire, stoked up by the servants before they left, was roaring gently away, and the iron plates of the range were red – and in places even white-hot. A servants' fire! They were always the best. It filled the large, bare, clean-scrubbed room with the ruddy glow that radiated through its thick iron bars, themselves red hot and so merged with it; and the copper pans and ladles twinkled on the opposite walls. Lucy and Theresa sat on one of the clean white tables, and Ursula settled herself in the cook's high-backed chair.

'Do you like it here, darlings?' said Ursula. She spoke in their native tongue, but softly; for there might be someone outside, and she did not assume, as English people are apt to do, that one may be sure of not being understood when one speaks one's own language in a foreign country.

'M-m,' said Theresa. 'It's not so bad. But I'm afraid the young man with the dark hair has fallen in love with me.'

'Oh!' said her sisters laughing. 'What makes you think so, sweetheart?' said Lucy.

'Oh, the way he looks at me. And he talks so much, my head swims and I don't always understand. So I just smile.'

'Oh, oh.' The sisters were terribly amused. 'The cunning of the child!' said Ursula to Lucy. 'Yes,' nodded Lucy. 'As if she didn't know that were the way to make him quite crazy.' 'But remember,' said Ursula, 'don't lead him on too far. We leave here immediately after twelve.'

'Oh, but,' said Theresa gaily, 'surely that's the very reason why I need not bother about him at all.' She had raised her voice a little, and Lucy laid a restraining hand on her arm.

'Oh,' said Theresa, 'for his sake, you mean.' She pouted and her fine eyebrows went up at the ends. 'For him, it is worth while. He is a poet, and he says he values experience for itself, not for what it leads to.'

'He will have a chance of proving that,' said Lucy darkly.

'Yes, indeed he will,' said Ursula.

'But I don't think the English are cold,' broke in Theresa again. 'I think that must be a story.'

'He is a poet,' Lucy reminded her. 'Poets are never cold. Remember Lord Byron.' She pronounced the name in the French fashion.

'My poet is not a bit like Lord Byron,' Theresa said proudly. 'He met me in the dark somewhere, during that last game; and after that, he kept ever so close to me, I thought he must be the one who was going to do the murder. I knew, if he had to murder someone, it would certainly be me. But no: he never even touched me with his hand, except to steady me on the stairs. He is passionate in words only, not in deeds.'

'Perhaps that is like an Englishman,' said Lucy.

'Or a poet,' said Ursula. 'But don't be too sure of him. The night is still young.'

'There is still hope,' said Theresa wickedly. 'Perhaps he may summon up courage to kiss me, before I go. I should like to be kissed by an English poet… But alas! the English have so many great poets, they have to be always quoting from them. Especially about love. They seem to get more pleasure out of that than out of the reality. To make it worse, my poet can quote from the ancients too: Sappho, Catullus, Martial. He intoxicates himself with words, trying to find the right ones to express me. And when I have gone, he will remember he didn't even kiss me.'

'Our little sister is growing up,' said Lucy meditatively, 'Soon we shall have to give her a dagger with the silver hilt, like yours and mine.' She opened the small vanity-bag she carried, and drew out the dagger she spoke of. It gleamed red from tip to handle, in the rays of the fire.

'She won't need it yet,' said Ursula. 'Her looks will protect her, for they are like snow.'

'Snow melts very quickly in the sun,' said Lucy sombrely.

'Then her protection must still be our affair, for she cannot have the dagger until she is eighteen. It was our mother's wish; and until then the responsibility is mine. Perhaps by then she will have a husband.'

'Let us hope so,' said Lucy sighing.

'Amen,' Theresa smiled. 'But see that you find me one who talks as well as the English poet, though not perhaps so much, or I won't have him. I will bide my time, like you.' She turned on Lucy. 'Why have you brought your dagger to the party? Ursula hasn't brought hers, and yet she is wearing her diamonds.'

Ursula laughed. 'Why, you silly child, you don t think I would use my dagger on someone who tried to steal my diamonds? In England, where the police do all that for nothing, and won't let anyone else? Why, they would put me in prison if I so much as scratched a man or stabbed his hand!'

'But if he took your diamonds?'

'They would get them back or give me new ones. In any case, that is not what our mother gave us the daggers for. It was to protect our honour and our lives, not a handful of shining pebbles.'

'But we had plenty then!'

'We have plenty now,' said Ursula. 'We shall never be short of things like those. We have good friends still, who have looked after us and always will. It is our business to keep our race pure. That is what we are left on this earth for, when all the others are gone. It is to your children, and to Lucy's and – who knows? – perhaps even to mine, that the world will look, some day, for leaders out of its present morass. We must never, never think of vengeance. We must forget the past, and fix our eyes on the future. If we do that, all will be well.'

'But our husbands!' said Theresa. 'Where are they to come from, if the race is to be kept pure? Our cousin Miklos is the only one left of our family, and I shouldn't care to marry him! Why, he's a half-wit, not a quarter as handsome, nor a millionth part as clever as—'

'Your English poet,' said Lucy. 'Why, Ursula, I believe the child is in love with him already!'

'No,' said Theresa. 'But I *should* like him to kiss me, once, before I leave.' She slipped off the table. 'I think I'll go now, and join in the game. Perhaps it's not such a silly game, after all. At any rate, it's silly to sit here, when we have come to a party. *Au revoir.*' She walked off slowly, with feline grace, to the door.

'Shall I stop her?' said Lucy, when they were left alone.

'No,' said Ursula. 'I think she was only teasing us; and that would make her wild. It would be better to watch the man; though from what she says, I don't think him very dangerous. But with these people, you never know. He has already seduced her mind with his poetry. He may be cunning as well as clever, and she is beautiful but not yet wise.'

'If I follow him he will suspect me,' said Lucy. 'But I could get someone else, someone he wouldn't suspect, to watch him. Someone who will do anything I ask.'

'What!' said Ursula. 'Has someone here fallen in love with you as well?'

'No,' said Lucy sombrely, 'it's not love. He knows who we are.'

Ursula looked up, startled.

'The sculptor-woman has given us away? To whom?'

'No. Don't be afraid. It was Markakis, the one who played. He recognized us. He has seen pictures.'

'And you didn't deny it?'

'No. He has insight. One could not lie to him, and be believed. He is as faithful as a dog. Also he is drunk, and I think angry. He would kill, if you gave him the word.' She held out her hand, with the shining dagger lying along the palm; its slender, bevelled point protruded beyond her fingers.

'Well, don't you give him *that*,' said Ursula drily, 'or the English police won't have far to look. I hear they are not all fools – nor always discreet and accommodating.'

'Oh, we shall be too far away for them to see us. We shall be a mere speck in the clouds by dawn to-morrow,' said Lucy, indifferently. 'But it will not come to that. I shall just give him the word, so that no harm shall come to our darling.' She put the dagger back in her bag. 'It must be nearly time for the scream.' She glanced at the china clock on the kitchen wall. 'These games are going to get longer and longer each time. Already this one has lasted ten minutes longer than the first. I see that people are beginning to seize on to the idea. I shall go and find a place to put myself.'

She too sauntered to the door.

Ursula stayed by the fire, musing and swinging her satin toe, until the scream – this time a woman's – rang out. Then she in her turn left the kitchen, and quietly closed the door.

When the lights went up the three sisters were on different floors.

## 13

Marcus Praed had them all assembled round him; and he sat, more like a judge than a detective, with his big red hands folded, and his big head thrown back, asking his slow, deliberate questions as if the answer really mattered and every word counted. This was how he did everything. It was the secret of his great popularity, for it flattered the company in which he happened to be with the belief that their little concerns were his main interest, at any rate for the time; whereas not even this much was true. Claribel watched him with a mixture of impatience at his ponderous pose, and pride in him because he was hers and the company were, as usual, hanging on his lips. Claribel was the corpse.

She knew perfectly well who had murdered her; so that the questioning bored her, as she was naturally not allowed to speak. She thought it a mean, spiteful trick, and she meant to get her revenge before long – perhaps not this evening; she hadn't time; but later a chance would come. She had been getting on so well, enjoying herself, reaching her objective… She had managed to sever Desmond from the Peggy-child who was pursuing him, and drag him, in pretended bacchanal playfulness, by the wrists up the stairs, away from all the others for a little while into one of the bedrooms. She had made him sit down beside her on a couch, had stroked his hair and given him a baby kiss or two; the others followed them, and there were several people soon in the room, but this didn't matter, no one could see, and in a way it was better so, because the minute the scream went off, she would have to get out of her compromising position; and this was difficult if they were a long way from the rest, since there might not be time to rejoin them while the corpse counted ten, but it was much easier if there were others in the room, because one could join another group or crawl along the floor to the other side, and who could tell where one had come from or whom one had been with? Desmond, of course, would do the crawling; she would sit there and powder her nose, and the lights would find her unruffled... Desmond was beginning to respond; his breath was coming faster, and the nape of his neck was hot and damp where she stroked it. He was a school-boy longing to prove himself a man, wax in her hands – melting wax. He had just seized her roughly to him, and was beginning to kiss her in earnest when, from behind, two hands closed, none too gently, round her soft little neck – and she realized that she was in the embarrassing position of being the corpse.

The worst of it was, Desmond didn't realize what had happened. The murderer had crawled quickly and silently away, and Desmond, in the middle of a kiss, wouldn't let her go. She tried to beat him off, but she had been tempting him for too long; and he naturally ignored her sudden change. Probably he had read that women are like that, and you must on no account take any notice of them... It was ridiculous. Even when the kiss was over, she still had to poke and prod him in a vain attempt to get him to go. She couldn't explain, with the murderer a few feet away, no doubt greedily listening. She couldn't utter the smallest whisper without betraying herself. And the seconds were ticking away and if at the tenth she didn't scream, her malicious friend, who too was doubtless counting, would have the laugh of her, and could even expose her before the company, when the detective asked his questions, by some apparently innocent remark... At the last moment, when all her efforts to send away Desmond had failed, she herself got up, slipped out of his grasp, and – afraid to cross the floor lest her murderer was lying in wait for her to trip her up as she passed – she made a dive for the bed, which luckily made less noise than beds usually do when jumped upon, and, hoping that the sound of her descent on it was covered by the scuffling going on in the corner by the door, at last, with deep relief, she opened her mouth and screamed.

When the lights went up, and Marcus came in to survey the scene, she found that most of the company had made their way to this room. There was poor foolish Desmond, looking very hot and rumpled, still glued to the couch; there were Markakis and Theresa, standing near the door; there were Sylens, Peggy and two other men in a heap on the floor. Carraway and Lucy were discovered wandering about the corridor below, with Betty and several other disconsolates not far away. In the basement were only Ursula, and the fat boy with his Junoesque wife who had been nagging at him, to judge by his appearance. Marcus looked carefully round the bedroom, counted them very deliberately, pointing a finger at each, and then released them. Claribel did not think he had noticed anything: her flop on the bed, if the others had heard it, would pass as the natural act for a corpse who knew the whereabout of her own bed and the hardness of her own floors.

Silly Desmond! She must warn him, before the next game, and arrange a signal. But these things never happen twice in the same way. Marcus's questions seemed completely impartial; but then, with Marcus, one never knew.

## 14

'Now,' said Marcus deliberately, 'where were you, Peggy, when the scream occurred? And please remember you must speak the truth, unless you are the murderer.'

'I was in a heap on the floor,' giggled Peggy happily.

'Where I found you. How long had you been there?'

'Oh, a minute. I had just come in, and someone grabbed my ankle and I fell down on top of several other people.'

Claribel tapped her foot. How like Marcus to concentrate his heavy attention on someone negligible! In the past, his unexpectedness had been for her his great charm; otherwise how could she have tolerated anyone for so long? But to-night she felt curiously perceptive: she seemed to be seeing right through everybody, including herself, whether she wished it or not. And she saw Marcus, not as her devoted lover of twelve years standing, a man who stood like a rock among the shifting sands of her existence, but as he really was: a profound, cold, soulless egoist, who was using her, as a scientist uses a living specimen, to prove or disprove a theory. He had gone through all the gestures, made all the speeches, of a man violently and unalterably in love; yet had she ever been quite convinced? He had written her letters which had made her tingle from head to foot with joy and fear, letters that cut like a whip-lash, letters that burnt themselves on to her brain. And yet, behind them all was still another man, who stood with folded arms watching the drama, awaiting the solution. She had always felt the mystery of Marcus; yes, even when he had bored her, as he did sometimes with his weighty talk. But she knew that she would never get rid of him; if they ever parted, it would be because *he* had had enough – he had found the answer to the problem and chose to sweep the pieces off the board back into their box. Of all the men who had loved her, he was the only one she feared.

'Hm,' said Marcus. 'Did anyone pass you in the corridor, on your way to the bedroom?'

'Oh yes,' said Peggy, 'several people.'

'Going or coming?'

'Going, I think.'

'How long before the scream?'

'Oh! I don't know. Not *just* before.'

'Five, ten seconds before?'

'More than that, I think,' said Peggy vaguely, not used to thinking in exact measurements.

'In your opinion, before the murder, therefore?'

There were cries of 'Not in order,' 'Inadmissible.'

'You're not bound to answer that, Peggy,' said Carraway. 'Only questions of fact.'

Marcus, with a grin, bowed his submission to their ruling. 'I didn't know that detectives had to conform to any rules,' he said blandly, 'except mentioning names.' He turned to Theresa. 'How long had you been standing where I found you?'

'A very little while.'

'Where had you come from?'

'From downstairs.'

'Did *you* pass anyone on your way?'

'Oh,' said Theresa, 'I should think I must have passed *every*body.' They all laughed.

Marcus looked the company carefully over. They had closed in on him a little; by now they were all interested in watching him at work.

'Let me go over the ones who have a complete alibi,' he said. 'You, Ursula, are quite outside suspicion. You had apparently spent a happy twenty minutes by the kitchen fire.'

Ursula smiled admission.

'And you, George and Dione,' to the fat boy and his wife, 'and you, Jack,' to Carraway; 'and Lucy' – he enumerated them one by one – 'you are all certain you never reached the top storey?'

They all said yes.

'By the way,' he jerked round sharply, 'where were you, Gilbert? I don't remember seeing you.'

Gilbert, unused to having attention focused on him, nevertheless bore it very well. He thought for a moment and said: 'I was on the stairs, between the first and second floors.'

'Going up or coming down?'

'Going up.'

'Did anyone pass you?'

Gilbert thought again, and said, 'No.'

'Now, you, Markakis. You had been standing by Theresa. For how long?'

'I had just come there.' Markakis looked the picture of slyness.

'From where?'

'From the other side of the room.'

Claribel's glance flickered at him. Surely he wasn't going to tell the truth! His leer, his dark hair falling in a lock over his low forehead, and the way his glazed eyes narrowed as he spoke, gave him a look of villainy mixed with impudence that filled her with misgiving. Oh, if he let her down! Let him try it – she would pay him out all right. She feared, however, that he was too drunk to care. Catching her warning glance, he returned it with a wider leer, and leaned forward purposefully, waiting for Marcus's next question.

'You moved *after* the scream, then, not before it?'

'Of course.'

'Then you were quite close to the scene of the crime?'

'Rather.'

'And you heard the body fall?'

'Yes.'

'Where were you when that happened?'

'I was lying on the ground, at the foot of the settee.'

'In front of it, or behind, by the window?'

'In front, between the settee and the bed.'

Claribel dug her nails into the palms of her hands. The little beast! Spying! So he had heard everything that there was to hear. She had actually stepped, or jumped over him when she dived on to the bed. No wonder she had been aware that she must not walk. But why was he telling the truth? She felt she would like to protest that he was not observing the rules of the game; but of course she could not, first because she was the corpse, second because she would give herself away, third because there *was* no such rule. Why had no one ever thought of that?

The murderer was not *obliged* to lie; he could if he chose. All the same, she was indignant: it was unsporting, somehow, for the murderer to assist the detective. If everybody did that, the game would be spoilt, not worth playing. And why, since Markakis chose to help him, didn't Marcus give up the farce of further investigation: name Markakis and let them get on to the next game?

'You heard the corpse fall,' went on Marcus imperturbably. 'Then what did you do?'

'I crawled away a few feet, and waited.'

'Oh!' cried the company. 'Stool-pigeon!' shouted someone, and they all laughed. Markakis bared his teeth at them. Marcus said blandly:

'I didn't know I had an unofficial assistant. Evidently Johnny was doing a little private detection.'

'Making up for the previous game,' said Claribel, 'when he had to give up his turn.'

All laughed again, except Ursula and Theresa who merely smiled, and Lucy, who remained grave.

'Well,' said Marcus, 'this is splendid. The corpse was murdered over there in that corner, and you were lying across his path of retreat. Now did *you* notice anyone pass you, or step over you?'

'Oh, certainly,' said Markakis. 'We collided in the dark.'

'And you, Desmond,' said Marcus. 'Had you been long on the settee?'

'I-er,' stammered poor Desmond. 'Yes,' he said desperately. 'I had been there all the time.'

'So *you* didn't collide with Markakis – with anyone, I mean – in the dark?'

'Er-no.'

'And did *you* hear the corpse flop on to the bed? You must have done.'

'Yes.'

'What did you do?'

'I stayed where I was.'

Marcus turned back to Markakis. 'How long between the flop and the scream?'

'Just one split second,' said Markakis cheerfully.

'Ah,' said Marcus. 'That's strange.' The company had gone curiously silent. They began to be aware that something more was going on than met the eye. Marcus added thoughtfully, 'For, you see, it means that the deceased was murdered some ten seconds *before* she flopped. I'm not sure if that's quite in order, you know. I hadn't thought of it before, but I understood that there was a rule that the corpse had to stay still as soon as murdered. I didn't know that the flop, as well as the scream, could be delayed.'

Claribel could restrain herself no longer. 'Why are you assuming that Markakis is speaking the truth?' she said exasperatedly. 'And if he's not, you have the answer, so why waste time?'

'S-sh,' said Marcus, wagging his finger. 'Dead women tell no tales,' and Dione, the fat boy's wife, drawled kindly, 'Oh, we all know Claribel. She was looking for a soft spot to lay her well-upholstered form – and I for one don't blame her. If anyone murders me, I shall do the same. That is, unless my fat husband is around – then there'll be no problem.'

The company, grateful for the diversion, laughed, but somewhat uneasily. The joke was a little too feeble to bridge the difficulty. Marcus waited for silence, and continued:

'Well, I think we must be firm and establish the rule, quite indubitably and without exceptions, that a corpse must lie where he or she falls. Otherwise the detective's work, difficult already, becomes impossible. Agreed?'

'Agreed,' they chorused with false heartiness.

'No allowances, even for Claribel. Well – but I'm afraid I've exceeded my time?'

'You have,' said Claribel spitefully. 'You will have to pay a forfeit now, even if you guess correctly.'

'What about it?' said Marcus. 'Shall I stop, or is it your pleasure that I continue?'

'Go on,' several voices called out.

'All the same,' said Marcus, 'I think it's time I summed up, before you all lose patience. One last question, Theresa. You say a number of people passed you on your way upstairs. Now tell me, did any of these pass you on the last flight of stairs, that is to say, between the first and second floors, or in the corridor outside the fatal bedroom?'

'Yes,' said Theresa.

'How many? Were you able to tell?'

'Yes.'

'How many, then?'

'Only one.'

'Going away?'

'Yes. Going away.'

'Man or woman?'

Interest was tense again. Theresa's calm equalled that of Marcus and, like his, was beautiful to see, but in a different way.

'It was a man,' she answered composedly.

'You are certain? How?'

'Because he wore a wrist-watch with a luminous dial.'

'All those with luminous watches hold up their hands,' commanded Marcus.

They did so: George, Desmond, Gilbert, Sylens.

Marcus looked them over carefully. 'Any women?'

'Yes, I,' said Betty. She had been silent for so long that her voice sounded queer to herself and to the others.

'You see, Theresa,' said Marcus, 'the wearing of a luminous wrist-watch is not necessarily the mark of a man.'

'Oh, but it *was* a man,' Theresa insisted.

'How do you know? No doubt you are right, but I want proof, not theory.'

'He smelt of smoke.'

'That's nothing. Dione, Peggy, Claribel – they all smoke like furnaces. You must give me a better reason.'

Theresa, who was herself smoking a cigarette, took a few leisurely breaths of it before she answered.

'I had my hands outstretched,' she said, 'and I touched him as he went by. I ran my hand along his coat-sleeve.'

'No one came past you back into the room?' said Marcus.

'No. I had only just come when there was the scream, and the lights went up.'

'I see. And was the person who collided with you, Markakis, wearing a wrist-watch?'

'I didn't notice. He may have been.'

'Now when the lights went up, Desmond and Sylens were in the room. And George, Dione, had never left your side?'

'Not he,' said Dione. 'You can take that as read, for this and all the other games.'

Marcus put his chin on his hand and mused. At last he raised his head.

'I give it up,' he said, suddenly and surprisingly. 'Or if you like, I'll risk the guess that Theresa was mistaken, and the murderer was Markakis.'

'But the wrist-watch!' they clamoured, disappointed. 'She can't have been.' And then, realizing that the game was over, some of them turned to Markakis. '*Did* you do it?'

Markakis, slowly, smilingly, shook his head.

'Desmond? Sylens?'

They both denied it. 'I see,' said Marcus gravely, still presiding, 'you don't give the same weight as I do to Theresa's man on the stairs.' He got up. 'I was assuming that he and the murderer were identical. That's where I lost my way.' He walked out of the room.

Then, slowly, the answer began to dawn on them, one by one, as it had already some minutes ago dawned on Claribel. Carraway was the first to see it, and turn away. He began an ostentatious conversation with Lucy and Ursula, while Sylens, who had been jealously watching Theresa, joined her.

'Who was it?' he said to her in a fierce undertone. 'Whose coat-sleeve did you touch in the dark?'

'I don't know.' Theresa's dimple appeared, though the smile was less on her lips than in her eyes. 'He wasn't *you*, that's all I could discover.'

Sylens' face lit up, and he drew in his breath sharply. He was no longer even mildly interested in the answer.

'Well, come on, someone,' said Peggy loudly, 'you can't walk out on us after all that. Isn't there a rule that the murderer must confess? Can anyone else have a pop, now Marcus hasn't found him? I say it was Desmond.'

'No, Peggy, it wasn't I,' said Desmond, unhappily. 'I've already told you.'

'Then who was the other guy with the luminous watch? I know – Gilbert! Why hasn't anyone asked Gilbert?'

Claribel, in anguish, looked from the little busy-body – whom what madness had induced her to invite? She would gladly have murdered *her* if she could – to her dark, silent husband.

Gilbert said slowly, in his usual low, aristocratic murmur, 'You are right, Peggy: it was I. Out of the mouths of babes and sucklings –' His laugh, though harsh, was, as always, restrained. 'You must admit I make a good murderer. Nobody thinks of me. I was lucky to have the chance of telling my lies, about going up, not down, the stairs, and passing no one...' His voice took on a slightly spiteful edge. 'Theresa did well to identify me as I went by. Perhaps she was looking for someone.' Theresa and Sylens had walked away to the end of the room and did not hear; but Lucy did, and Gilbert was unaware of the look that passed between her and Ursula. He went on in his thin, spiteful voice: 'Perhaps Desmond could tell us what was the reason for the short interval between the fall and the scream…'

But of all those who had been gathered round Marcus, only Claribel, Markakis and the ever-interested Peggy remained to hear that last murmured phrase.

Marcus re-entered, smiling, ruddy and glowing like the midnight sun. 'Well, who was it?' he said, rubbing his hands. 'Has he owned up? Gilbert? Well, well, of course! How slow I am.'

'Oh, what a shame!' cried Peggy. 'I believe you knew it all the time!'

'Oh, come, come,' said Marcus gaily. 'Would I deceive you and waste your time?… Well, are we having another game, or must we soon assemble for supper? I've been outside. It's a wonderful night, so cold and clear. A turn up and down the lane would do you all good before the meal, and I'm sure Gilbert and Claribel will be glad to get rid of us. Lucy, will you join me in a stroll up – or rather down – the garden-path?'

He gave her his arm.

## 15

Lucy and Marcus walked along the pathway, winding and hedged with holly, of Claribel's garden.

'See here!' said Marcus, stooping down. 'Here are some Christmas roses. Do you like them? They are my favourite flower.' He took out his penknife. 'It's tiresome of Claribel not to have kept them covered with glass, as I asked her to do when I gave her the root twelve months ago. But the hedge has sheltered them.' He cut the stiff white flowers, one by one, and bound them together with a piece of thin wire which he drew from another pocket.

'Will you wear them?' he said. '"Christmas roses, pure and pale." They become you, and you them. Don't forget, I am giving you the flower I love best.'

Lucy let him pin the flowers into her coat. She said nothing, for there was no way that did not sound waspish of expressing what she thought; and to sound waspish would be to sound concerned.

'Claribel will be annoyed,' he said, 'when she finds the flowers all gone – cut out from the centre. You see, it's all very significant and allegorical, what I'm doing. Are you not a little intrigued?' And when she still did not answer, he added, 'At least, you can follow my meaning. That is a welcome novelty, for me.'

Lucy thought it best to change the subject. She said, 'You have a strange sense of humour, haven't you?'

'In what way?' Marcus sounded genuinely surprised.

'You told me you were not above taking revenge,' said Lucy. 'But I didn't think you would choose so petty a form of it.'

'Oh, that!' His voice was all candour. 'I assure you, my dear girl, you misjudge me. I had no idea where my questions were leading until the very end. It was your sister Theresa who gave me my clue. I thought it was that young devil Markakis until she mentioned the man with the wrist-watch, who passed her on the stairs. Of course, I found it strange that Markakis should tell the truth, if he were the murderer. The natural thing for him to have said was that he had just come in. I was puzzled by that; and also, of course, by the way he was giving his evidence. He was obviously full of malice, and cram-full of inner knowledge. In short, he knew why there was only "one split second" as he called it, between the flop and the scream. I don't think he knew who did the murder. Perhaps he thought it was Desmond. He is drunk, and for some reason angry with Claribel, but I give him the credit of believing that he wouldn't go to such lengths–'

'Why?' said Lucy, innocently. 'Would her husband mind? I thought he knew and acquiesced in things of that kind.'

Marcus gave a low laugh. 'Ah, you go by logic! But human nature is not logical, my dear girl. It is just because Gilbert accepted *me* – made his great sacrifice for Claribel's sake – that he will not tolerate a new-comer. Claribel persuaded him once, that someone else was essential to her happiness. Was it her fault, she said with tears in her eyes, if she had found this out too late? Gilbert must understand. She is a great hand at getting others to understand. But do you imagine that after making such an effort, he is going to repeat it, again and again, when repetition makes him, not noble and self-sacrificing, but merely ridiculous? For we all want something back, you know, even if it's only to be allowed to shine... I wonder whether it was by chance he was there – whether he followed Claribel from habit, or whether he was suspicious; and if the latter, what made him so. Ah well! It's proving an eventful evening for all of us in one way or another.'

They came to the end of the path, and stood looking out across the river. Here there was a light mist, and the cold smell of water and rotting leaves.

'Claribel's punt is in the boat-house,' he said, 'and opposite us is an island. Shall I ferry you across? There is a little log house, and I would light you a fire. We should be so much better there than at the stupid party.'

Lucy said, 'I should like to. I should like to escape from the stupid party, and from myself as well. But you see, I can't. I can no more do the one than the other.'

'One *can* do anything one wants to,' said Marcus quietly, 'if one wants it sufficiently.'

'Then prove it.'

'How?'

'Make me forget – who I am, and where I came from. If I could do that, I could escape my destiny, which is – to return.'

Marcus took her in his arms and kissed her.

'Well,' he said at last, 'is it achieved?'

She sighed. 'No. No. I must go back. But listen: you have given me the Christmas roses. Well, when we get to the door of the house, I shall give *you* something in exchange: on one condition – that you don't examine it until the party is over. By that time I shall be – many miles away. But on the thing I shall give you, you will find my name, and where I live. You are a great traveller. If you like adventure, bring it to me. If you don't, then keep it as a souvenir. Remember, there are no promises on either side: if you don't want to come, it's your affair. If you come, and I don't choose to remember you, that's my affair. What do you say?'

He was silent, thinking.

'Or,' said Lucy, 'if you prefer the short run, I will come over to your island. But then, I keep my gift.'

Marcus said calmly, 'I choose the long run.'

'You prefer the future to the present?'

'Always.'

'Even though the future may never come?'

'Yes – even then.'

'I think,' said Lucy, 'no one here would agree with you. But I do.'

At the door of the house she gave him the silver dagger.

## 16

The scene between Gilbert and Claribel was short and sharp. It took place in their bedroom. When Claribel saw that it had to be, she took him there; and shutting the door and leaning against it, as if it were she who barred his way, she opened fire. By now, she had worked herself into a fury; for it was her great gift that, though she herself acknowledged no laws of conduct, she could always think of those that applied to other people; and it never took her a moment to convince herself that she was right. Thus she spoke always with the vehemence of conviction; and it was rarely that she failed to put her opponent to flight with this weapon. Already she had Gilbert on the defensive; a sense of guilt, very familiar, was already creeping over him, as he stood before her.

'Now,' she snapped, her eyes blazing, 'explain yourself, please. Explain why you chose to make a fool of me before all those people.'

Gilbert opened his mouth to speak, but her high voice easily drowned his habitual murmur.

'You followed us,' she said. 'You had been there all the time. You knew what happened, and you have such a mean, suspicious, petty mind that even now, although you know me, although I've proved to you a hundred times that I wouldn't condescend to be to you –' Her breath failed her for a moment, or else she had lost her way in the sentence. At any rate Gilbert was able to murmur:

'I wasn't suspicious. I never thought.'

'Then why did you follow me?'

'Well,' said Gilbert, 'haven't I the right even to do that? They all left the ticket with murderer on it, so I had to take it. I followed you because I couldn't think of anyone else to murder.'

'You were pretty secretive about it, anyway,' said Claribel, relaxing a little, as she realized that she had won already. 'Why did you hide behind us on the settee?'

'I didn't,' said Gilbert, 'at least, I didn't realize till I touched you that you had Desmond there. I put out my hand and I felt a man's arms round you. I thought it was Marcus, and then I remembered Marcus was the detective. So I saw red. I mean, I was carried away. I wanted, for one thing, to know who it was... I couldn't help it, Claribel.'

Claribel regarded him with contempt: what a poor creature he was, apologizing already! Five minutes ago, among the others, he had had her almost scared. She had expected to fight, to have to use her wits; but it was a walk-over!

'I see,' she said. 'And so you had to lead Marcus on, and on, so that the whole crowd should know what you knew. You couldn't have come and asked *me*, for instance, what had happened? How could I help it if that silly boy caught me in the dark? He had been trying to, all evening; and I thought I had given him the slip. And then – what do you suppose *I* could do? Did you expect me to stand up and scream? As it was, I had all I could do to get away... And that was through you, you, you,' she screamed, her fury rising again. 'You are insufferable. I won't stand it, I can't *bear* the humiliation. Even Marcus was laughing at me. And Markakis, odious little beast. And those women! Theresa was in the room. She will tell her sisters what they haven't gathered already; it will be a fine story for them to take home. I shall be a laughing-stock. You have ruined my career. Think of their connexions! I could have got half the crowned heads of Europe through them.'

'Oh, I don't know,' said Gilbert doubtfully. 'I shouldn't worry about them, Claribel. They'll put it down to me, not you. I was jealous. I thought you liked kissing that vulgar, pimply little brute. I thought it was you who had got him there.'

'There you go again,' cried Claribel. 'Just because he is an actor, he must be common and vulgar, according to you. And pimply! He has a Greek profile. I intend to make a mask of him, and I intend that he shall pay for it too, or rather his mother who dotes on him will. You never think of my interests, you never think at all, except of yourself and what's owing to you. It's you who have the common, commercial mind.'

'There's Marcus,' murmured Gilbert. 'I did what you wanted over *him*.'

'Yes. And now I have to be eternally grateful to you for your nobility in doing something which you couldn't help doing, which nobody asked you to do, which you did of your own free will.' She realized there was some discrepancy here, but she hurried past it. 'You said you would rather have me on those terms than not at all. You said you couldn't live without me. Well, if you want to back out of the bargain, you know what to do. Marcus and I won't mind.'

'*You* may not,' said Gilbert, a note of spite creeping into his thin voice again.

'What do you mean?' said Claribel, arrested.

'Oh, nothing. But twelve years is a long time. It seems to me, Marcus has played his cards pretty cleverly. It was easy for him to make protestations, after all. He knew he could count on *me* – to play the complaisant fool.'

Claribel came close up to him, her eyes narrowed, her small white teeth bared.

'Are you suggesting,' she said, 'that Marcus is a liar, too? That he never meant to marry me if you got out of the way? If so, I congratulate you. It must be wonderful to have a mind like yours, so that when your miserable little dignity is offended, you can always dredge up some mean idea to throw at the other person.'

'I didn't say that,' said Gilbert, receding a step, but a step only. 'I merely said, twelve years is a long time, Marcus is a dark horse. You've long since given up watching him. You think you don't need to. Your natural vanity makes you blind. But *I* watch him always, for your sake as well as mine. He can deceive you. He's used to it. He could always deceive anybody he set out to. But he never bothers about me – he has no reason to. The onlooker sees most of the game.'

'What are you hinting at?' cried Claribel. 'Out with it. What do you know, that you are hiding? You're all up to something. I feel as if I were surrounded by enemies and spies. What has he told you? Has he found out –'

'What?' said Gilbert, holding his ground.

'Oh, nothing.' Claribel recovered herself quickly. 'Thanks to you, of course, he knows – about Desmond. But I shall speak to him and explain. And Gilbert, if you don't do something – I don't care what, that's your affair – to alter the impression you have created, I won't go on. I won't stay. The party can go to blazes –'

'Oh come, darling,' said Gilbert soothingly. 'You can't leave our guests – especially our distinguished guests. What will they think of English manners if we trail our private affairs under their noses? I was wrong. I'm sorry. I'll put it all right – fraternize with Desmond. They'll forget it in no time. I don't suppose they really gathered much, you know. We'll give them supper, and –'

'All right,' said Claribel. By now, she was tired of the discussion, and feeling cold. It was time to forgive Gilbert, loathsome as he had been. She put up her cheek to be kissed. 'Now I'll find Marcus and explain, and all will be as before. And if you want to do something to please me, the next time we play murder-party, find Markakis and give him –'

'A kick in the pants,' said Gilbert. 'I will. From you and me.'

'And don't blame poor Desmond. He is silly but he means no harm.' At the door she waved her hand to him and vanished.

'I don't,' said Gilbert; but not till she was out of hearing.

## 17

Ursula and Carraway sat by the fire, at one end of the long room, and talked. The others had all, apparently, accepted Marcus's idea of a walk before supper, except Peggy and Betty who were conversing in whispers by the fire at the other end of the room. Above, where the supper was being laid, heavy footsteps went to and fro, as Gilbert carried from the kitchen the dishes given him by Claribel.

Carraway said, 'I am frightened, Ursula. I am living at a *tempo* much too fast for me. I don't know if I can keep it up. And yet I'm elated. I feel as if I were rushing on to my destruction; and yet I can't stop, because I can't want to.'

Ursula answered, 'Yes. I can feel it too – the alarm, the fear you speak of. There is an influence at work in this house, a disintegrating one. When I came here, I was sure of myself, of my future. Now I am so no longer.'

'Where were you in the last game?' said Carraway. 'I was looking for you everywhere.'

'I was in the kitchen,' said Ursula. 'My sisters were there too, most of the time. And do you know, while we were all there together, I felt my old self again. I talked to them, I said the things we have so often spoken of together, about our duty to the race and to each other. And for a while I was happy. I thought I had re-found myself and them. But then I was gradually aware that their thoughts were elsewhere; that they were agreeing with their lips, but their hearts were turned away. Oh, little Theresa didn't even trouble to conceal it: she is a child, she can't understand. But my beloved second sister – she, who has always been the strongest of us all – something is happening to her as well. I can feel it. When she came here, she would have done murder for the idea we were pledged to defend. Now – the weapon has fallen from her fingers. Why? What is happening to us all?'

'Never mind,' said Carraway. 'Don't ask. Don't inquire. Think of the moment only. In a few hours short we shall have woken up maybe. Meanwhile forget your sisters, forget your race, forget everything except me. Race! Why should it matter to you what will happen when you and I are dust?'

'You say that,' murmured Ursula. 'You, a painter of trees! Why should it matter to you that the image of your trees should exist long after you are no more than a name, a signature on the corner of your canvas?'

'It doesn't,' said Carraway. 'I used to think it did, a little. But now I know it doesn't. I paint, as I love, because I can't help it. I am an instrument, on which someone or something plays a tune I don't know. No, not even a tune – merely a note or two towards some symphony, that is going on around me though I can't hear. At the moment, your note and mine are blending to make one chord.'

'But this is madness,' said Ursula, 'or rather, it is magic. What has happened to the solid world – to reality? Nothing seems to exist for me any longer, except this strange dark house, and the people in it. I should never have come here. *We* should never have come here, we three; or at least we should have clung together. I am lost, cut off from my background, my history. Is that possible? Is there any I, apart from the sum-total of my ancestry, and the play of my experience on that? Could I really begin again, like a seed blown by the wind for hundreds of miles across the sea – begin again on alien soil? What a relief it would be to be free!'

'You want to produce a hero,' said Carraway, 'a Siegfried, or a Joan of Arc maybe. But the living members of your race are all decadents and half-wits, or worse still, they have turned middle-class gentlemen in order to curry favour with the bourgeoisie. Forget them, and come with me.'

'But my sisters!' said Ursula.

'They can take care of themselves,' said Carraway, 'as well, or better, than you or I. To-night is the reality. The rest was false, a structure of your imagination only. That's why it is crumbling to pieces now. How soon will you believe me and come away?'

'Oh, I am weakening,' said Ursula. 'First Theresa, and then me. But Lucy is strong. She would despise me. She –'

'Then where,' said Carraway, 'do you think she is now?'

Ursula was about to answer, when the door at the far end of the room opened, and Lucy came in. She was very pale, but composed; she went and warmed her hands before the other fire. Ursula hurried towards her.

'Lucy!' she said. 'Dearest, where have you been?'

Lucy looked up at her unseeingly. 'I have been walking in the garden,' she said, 'with the explorer, Marcus Praed.'

'You too?' murmured Ursula.

Lucy stared back at her gravely. 'See here,' she said, 'he gave me these flowers, which they call Christmas roses. To him, they are the most beautiful of flowers. And I accepted them. You know what that means?'

Ursula shook her head. Her dark eyes were wide with what might have been alarm or expectancy.

'You should,' said Lucy, 'for it was you who taught it me. In our family, you said, there was a rule: a gift for a gift. And the thing given had to be at least ten times the value of the thing received. You told me that one of our ancestors almost ruined himself because his wife accepted a string of diamonds from someone he considered his inferior in rank – for of course, even *we* took gifts from our superiors.'

'Our equals,' corrected Ursula gently.

'Well, I held myself technically bound by that rule,' went on Lucy imperturbably. 'And I have given him – no, not myself, darling: I am not so vain.' She pressed her pale cheek against the cold flowers. 'I gave him – or lent him, it is for him to say – my silver dagger. If you had looked out, a quarter of an hour ago, you could have seen it changing hands. Since then I have been walking in the garden, wondering if I did well… You can't think how much lighter and happier I feel without it.' She looked Ursula straight in the eyes. 'I advise you to do the same.'

'And Theresa?' said Ursula. 'Is that your advice to her also?'

'Theresa!' said Lucy. Her look softened. 'Theresa will never need even to see hers,' she said. 'Life has never meant her to be bothered with such things as heirlooms. It has been seen to since her birth; and she is fortunate, and we must leave her alone.'

'I see,' said Ursula.

She kissed Lucy, and then she turned and walked slowly back to Carraway.

## 18

M arcus stood in the kitchen doorway, filling it with his great frame. Claribel looked up.

'Oh, there you are!' she cried joyously. 'I've been longing to see you for ages. Where have you got to, all evening? We seem hardly to have exchanged a word. Where is Gilbert, I wonder? Oh, here he comes!' Marcus stood aside to let Gilbert pass. 'Now listen, dear,' said Claribel, 'you carry on with the rest of these' – she indicated the table loaded with plates of cake and fruit and sandwiches – 'and I'll be down again presently. I want to talk to Marcus.'

Without a backward glance she led Marcus away, upstairs to her studio, which overlooked the garden.

'Here at least we shan't be disturbed,' she said, unlocking the door, and locking it again behind her. 'This was the one room that didn't get left open.' A great porcelain stove kept the room always warm. On the bench was a half-modelled face in clay, as yet unrecognizable. From the walls, like the heads of Bluebeard's wives, gazed down a melancholy row of models, some familiar to Marcus, some unknown.

'Have you finished your portrait of the three sisters? he said. 'May I see it?' He went purposefully towards one of the draped easels, but she checked him.

'No, no, it's not finished.'

'But they are leaving England – to-night, I believe.'

'Yes, but I have sketches. And there are photographs to help one out. Not that I shall need them.'

'Who are they, Claribel?' said Marcus, coming back to her. 'It seems as if one ought to know; but I never read society papers, and I have been away for so long.'

'Ah!' said Claribel, smiling with babyish malice, 'so you haven't found out *that*, for all your clever detective work! Don't ask me: I'm under solemn oath not to tell. They wish to be incognito – they would not have come otherwise. The whole house is surrounded, you know! Isn't it thrilling? And when they go, their car will take them immediately to a place where there will be a special aeroplane waiting to carry them off to – their home town. Of course, their country is not so important as it used to be. But they think its future rests with them, and they're pretty carefully guarded while they're here; so somebody else must think so too. Which do you like best? I like the youngest one, Theresa.'

'Ah, that requires consideration,' said Marcus. He sauntered up to the moulds, and stood for a moment in front of each, looking at them so attentively that Claribel became uneasy. She was just about to interrupt him when he turned to her with a smile.

'These things remind me,' he said, in his pleasant anecdotal voice, 'of a little cathedral I know in Wales. It was roofless and partly ruined until about the latter half of last century; and then, whoever restored it had a bright idea – one among many: along the top course of the outside south wall he arranged to have a row of projecting stone blocks, not very big, they appear to have a section of about nine inches square from where one sees them, but of course it may be more. And the end of each is carved into a head of one of the Kings or Queens of England; the whole series are there in chronological order, beginning with William the Conqueror, and he has even slipped in Oliver Cromwell. But the curious thing is,' he turned back again for a moment to the portrait moulds, 'that when he had done them all, down to the present day, he had only one block left. And there it stays, a blank, waiting to be carved. The villagers are mildly superstitious about it: they think that when the last block has been used there will be no more monarchs in England. Your row of moulds reminded me of that. I don't quite know why, for you have plenty of room for more – you could carry them all round the walls if you wished, couldn't you?'

'What do you mean?' said Claribel angrily.

'Oh, nothing, nothing. Just an association of ideas. It's always salutary,' he said, stopping again in front of his own mask, 'to see oneself as merely a member of a series. "What, will the line stretch out to the crack of doom?"'

'What are you getting at?' Claribel's colour had risen, and her breath came quickly. 'Gilbert was right, then, you *have* been listening to tales against me.'

'Not listening,' said Marcus mildly. 'Merely hearing. Well, I must own, I really haven't any cause for complaint. What you did once, you are entitled to do again. I suppose I should take it as a compliment to myself that you were moved to repeat the experiment. Yes, and it is a compliment, too, that you thought *me* worth deceiving, whereas poor Gilbert – Tell me, Claribel, what is your technique with Gilbert? I see such interesting possibilities.'

He sat down beside her, on a low bench, and spread out his large hands on his knees. Claribel watched him in fascinated fury.

'I mean, his situation interests me. Do you regard him as utterly safe and negligible, and so tell him the whole truth as it unfolds? If so, what is his ethical position – for instance, as regards me? Ought he not, as a good friend of mine, to have let me in on your affairs? No, I suppose not: his first duty is to you. He has therefore to be your accomplice. Rather awkward, for a gentleman! But then that's what I have always felt about having rules of conduct: what does one do, when two sets of rules are mutually contradictory?'

'Oh, do stop talking, said Claribel, 'and *say* something for a change. You! What right have you to criticize Gilbert? You love no one and nothing, except the sound of your own voice. You don't care what trouble and unhappiness you cause, and it's all in the name of what you call truth and abstract theory. If I conceal some things from Gilbert, it's because he has suffered enough, and I don't choose to hurt him any more. But you can't understand that. Go and tell him whatever it is you've heard, if you're not satisfied with the damage you've done already. We shall see if he will thank you as you deserve. I wish he would,' she added malevolently. 'I wish that for once he'd show himself master in his own house, and tell you never to come here again.'

Marcus stared at her in pretended surprise. 'You really mean that?' he said. 'You mean you will be glad if, when I say goodbye to you at the end of this party, it is for the last time?'

'Oh, I don't know, I don't know,' said Claribel, beginning to cry. 'I don't know what to think after the way you behaved this evening – exposing me in front of all those people. You had no right. I could have explained. You and Gilbert, you have infected each other: you have become suspicious towards me and mean, and he is trying to ape you and your possessiveness. I don't know which of you has been the more hateful…'

She moved closer to him, and nestled against his shoulder. 'Let's forget about it,' she said cajolingly, 'let everything be as it was before. What if Desmond did kiss me in the dark? You make such mountains out of mole-hills, you old stick-in-the-mud. It meant nothing at all, to me.'

'Maybe not,' murmured Marcus, 'but then, there are so many mole-hills. Added together, they almost make a mountain: Sylens, Carraway, Markakis I suppose, and God knows how many besides.'

Claribel laughed, carried away by her vanity, and misled by his gently humorous tone.

'Well. I can't help it, can I, if people fall in love with me? And anyway, all that is ancient history. It's all over and we are all good friends – except Markakis, spiteful little beast that he is. And you! You led him on – you played into his hands. He was longing for all that to come out, and you helped him.'

'My dear girl,' said Marcus, 'I assure you, I thought he was the murderer until the very end, and you saw how I stopped and went out immediately. I even tried to divert the rest of the company by suggesting a walk.'

'You didn't succeed,' said Claribel. 'Gilbert was furious. I had all I could do to pacify him this time. Of course, he knows nothing about anyone except you. But he was furious even about Desmond. I don't know what I shall do. If he goes on like that, I shall have to shake him off, after all. What do you say? Would you be pleased if I asked you to take me away? You see, between ourselves, darling, there are times when I'm a little bit afraid of Gilbert. He looks and speaks so queerly –'

Her hands were playing with Marcus's lapels, stroking his thick tweed coat, patting him gently. Marcus stayed perfectly still.

'I shouldn't do that,' he said calmly. 'You couldn't desert him after all he's done to please you. He lives for nothing else but you. If you left him he would kill himself, or just quietly die.' He knew that she believed this; whether it was true or not, he no longer cared. He knew that her vanity would accept it as a tribute, without further examination.

'Yes,' she said in a low voice, and with a seriousness that surprised him, for he did not remember ever to have heard it from her. 'But if I stay, he may kill me first.' She sat up, and brushed the fair hair back from her still youthfully smooth forehead. 'Marcus, suppose I tell you I mean that? Will you believe me? Will you take me away? You've said you would, many times…'

There was a long silence.

At last Marcus said, 'I'm afraid, my dear, you've left it too late – by several hours.'

She stared at him, unable to believe what she had heard. She put out one of her hands, against his chest, the better to see his face. For a moment she looked pathetic, forlorn, as if she were going to cry again. Then, as comprehension slowly came, her eyes narrowed.

'I see. So Gilbert was right. What has come over him this evening? He is inspired.'

Her hand, resting on his coat, felt something hard. Before he could stop her, she had turned the lapel outward. Sticking up above his breast-pocket was the handle of Lucy's dagger. She snatched it away.

'Where did you get this?' She glanced quickly at the blade. 'I see. So that's the answer.' She jumped up from the bench, holding the dagger behind her. 'That's why you wanted to know who they were – if it was true, that is, for you knew already. My God, how you can lie!'

Marcus remained seated. 'You had better give it me back, Claribel,' he said, 'I was merely taking care of it for the lady. I assure you, if it gets lost, I am responsible, and I should have no idea where to send my apologies, for I haven't even looked at it. That will show you how curious I am.'

'Liar!' said Claribel. 'If you haven't looked it's because you didn't know her name was on it. Did she give it to you, or did you steal it? I suppose she did. She must be pretty far gone then. You and your honeyed tales! What a success for you! How great a success you shan't know till they've gone. Until then, I'll keep this, and give it back to her. You are a fool, Marcus – nothing can come of it, you know.' She laughed. 'I shall love to see your face when the secret is revealed.'

Marcus rose slowly. The bench, and Claribel's modelling table, were between them. Behind her, a French window leading on to a flat leaded roof was ajar.

'Please let me have it,' Marcus said patiently, 'unless you want me to make myself really unpleasant.'

Claribel laughed again. 'What can you do? If you are thinking of making another scene before the company, let me tell you that I have only to call their car, which is waiting round the corner, and make up some story about a message by telephone, and your goddess will be immediately spirited away. What is more, Marcus, if I see you speak to her, or either of her sisters, in a way that can't be heard by us all – I *will*. You know me. I mean what I say.'

'Give me that dagger,' said Marcus. 'Don't play the fool.'

He pushed aside the bench and the heavy table so roughly that the half-modelled mask of clay fell to the ground. Claribel retreated.

'If you don't,' he said, his self-control suddenly snapping, 'I'll strangle you.'

Claribel stepped out on to the balcony. She was frightened, but malice drove her on. With one stride he was upon her. But before he could grasp her arm, she had thrown the dagger out and away, as far as she was able, into the shrubbery.

Marcus shrugged his shoulders.

'I shall go and fetch it,' he said. 'What a pity for you, you throw so badly. It might have gone into the river, and that would have been awkward for us all.'

He put his hands in his pockets and sauntered away.

Panic seized Claribel.

'Oh, Marcus, don't go, don't go!' she cried, running after him. 'I didn't mean it. I have the key.' She held it out to him, like a peace-offering. He looked down at it for a moment, and then took it without a word. With his other hand still in his pocket he strolled to the studio door and unlocked it.

'I shall be back in a few minutes,' he said.

He went out and closed the door. She heard the key turn in the lock on the other side.

Lost in astonishment, she stood in the middle of the studio, staring at the locked door. At last she turned and began slowly picking up the clay and the tools that had rolled off the table.

## 19

Claribel waited. Five minutes, ten, passed by.

She sat on the bench, forlorn, childlike, all her bravado gone. She was not thinking, except perhaps occasionally that Gilbert would have finished laying the table, and would probably come to see where she was, quite soon. It would be another grievance, that she had left him to do everything alone. Ordinarily he would not have resented this. But in his present mood it might make him still more peevish. Even he, little though he asked of her, required to be kept going with occasional doses of praise and a show of affection, if he was not to flag in his service. But this was only at the back of her mind; she could not bother to worry about it very greatly. In the chaos of her mind it was swept round like a straw in a whirlpool.

What was happening? Was this a nightmare, or was it really true – that she had lost Marcus for ever? For Gilbert, bitter though he was – and his bitterness was new and strange to her, like a sudden slap from a tender nurse from whom one has grown to expect nothing but warmth and love – Gilbert could, if she exerted all her strength, be won over. But Marcus, if he had changed, had changed for good. She recognized this by immediate perception. And if Marcus was lost, where was she? Half an hour ago it had seemed of no importance. She had actually intended to let him know how often, during the twelve years of their intimacy, he had bored her with his ponderous talk; and many other spiteful things she had meant to say, such as that she had found him slow even as a lover.

Humourless, thick-skinned, solemn, obtuse: she had thought of many hard words. Doubtless he would only have laughed; they had quarrelled before, and she had never before succeeded in making him really angry, until to-night. She knew this, because she had never before seen him like that: angry with her, not as herself the exasperating, but always adorable, Claribel; but as a *thing*, an obstacle that stood in his way; an enemy that had seized a chance to get the better of him, and whom he must defeat by guile.

Yes, that was it: an enemy. And suddenly she realized that in this house, which she had thought filled with her friends, she was surrounded by enemies. Marcus, Gilbert, Markakis, all turned against her; even Carraway and Sylens, if not hostile, at least not interested any more; and the rest, unknown quantities, probably indifferent, but with no great reason to take her side. What had happened? What had caused it? What influence was at work? And, above all, what madness had made her offend Marcus when most she needed his aid? If she had kept him, even his ordinary friendship, nothing else would have mattered. Marcus was an army in himself: whoever had him on his side need fear nothing, for he breathed strength, indomitable courage, and unshakable loyalty. He was a dissembler, he loved the game for its own sake. But he was no traitor; he did not play for his own gain, as smaller men can't help doing when they practise arts of dissimulation. He had his own rules, which he observed scrupulously, to please no one but himself.

And she could so easily have kept him. This passing fancy of his – it would *have* to be ephemeral, for in a few hours the three princesses would be snatched away, back into their own world out of which they had so strangely stepped at Claribel's instigation, and none of those present would ever see them again, except per-haps in the distance, from among a crowd... To-morrow Marcus would wake up, like Carraway and Sylens, and realize that these exotic creatures were not for them. And then they would return to her, Claribel, a little disillusioned perhaps, but resigned, and soon contented again. If only she hadn't made that fatal error, of defying him, of throwing away the dagger! She could have kept it, and teased him, and given it back to him in time.

Well, perhaps it would be all right still. The dagger hadn't gone far – it had fallen a few yards away, near the path, among the bushes. He might bear her a grudge for a while, but he was not mean: he would forgive her. He knew she was temperamental, impulsive; he had always found that amusing and attractive. He could not blame her too much for acting in character... He was a long time away – at least it seemed a long time. She went out on to the balcony and looked down. He was no longer there.

She heard the key turn in the lock. She stepped back into the room, all ready with her speeches of reconciliation and pleading. One look at his face arrested her.

He said, 'You have done famously. The dagger isn't there.'

She gasped. 'You couldn't find it? But I *know* where it fell just below. I saw it. I could find it blindfolded.'

'I know. I marked the spot, too. Also, I had a powerful torch. I did not say I couldn't find it. I said it was not there.'

'Give me the torch,' said Claribel.

She ran out of the room. Marcus slowly followed.

## 20

'And so,' said Sylens, 'after to-night, I shall never see you again?'

'I don't think so,' said Theresa.

'And you won't even tell me your name?'

'It would be no use if I did.'

'I don't understand,' said Sylens.

'You will, before long.'

Her voice was sombre. They were walking along the river bank. They had left Claribel's garden by the postern gate – for Sylens knew the way, and they wanted to avoid the others. He had wanted to get her away, out of Claribel's house and garden; but now, although they were alone, and freed from the constraint of walls and eyes, Sylens was aware that no spell was broken, no barrier removed. The sky was glittering with stars; the dark river eddied by, but silently. Suddenly there seemed nothing to say; and he, who had thought he could live in the present, was crushed by a sense of the future, of emptiness, of loneliness, that the darkness and the space seemed to enhance. In the warm room, with others nearby, he had been able to talk, to tease, to make love in a thousand ways, with looks and words and gestures. Now, he could think of nothing but that the minutes were ticking away, adding themselves up to make the quarters, the halves, the wholes of the remaining hours that were so few, one dared not name their number. And then, when she had stood there, on the path overlooking the river, and told him in her sombre voice that this time to-morrow she would be hundreds of miles away, it was to him as if the bottom had dropped out of his world. He could not see how he was ever to learn to bear life, if he never saw Theresa again.

'But why?' he said. 'Why?'

She would tell him nothing.

In the dim light he could see her pale profile and the downward droop of her lips. In her young voice there was sadness, but there was also a note of firmness, of determination; she knew her destiny, and that it was hard, but she did not ask, perhaps did not altogether wish, to escape it. She was sharing, perhaps for the first time, a little of her inmost self with a friend. A very little; but she would not have revealed even that much if she had not known for certain that there was to be no sequel. He was aware, and it hurt him, of what had gone into the making of her character: of the long training, the checking of every impulse, the instilling of mistrust. What could he, in a few hours, do against such formidable forces? Yet he knew that this quality of mistrust, which she and those who had taught it to her called restraint, poise, good breeding, was the essence of her beauty. He knew also – and this was the greatest torment of all – that it could be overcome, charmed away or swept aside: that she herself, if the whim seized her, would one day discard it. But not for him; he was a step on the way, not the goal. And this was just; he had done nothing, there was nothing in him, to deserve better.

Slowly they left the river, and walked back through the thin trees to the door of Claribel's garden.

Inside the garden it was darker; the great rhododendrons that edged the path shut out the light, except from immediately over-head, and enclosed them. One felt safer here, after all. His spirits rose.

'Theresa,' he said, almost sharply, and laid a hand on her arm.

She turned to him inquiringly. There still was nothing to say. They kissed instead. He was aware of the answering pressure, gentle but definite, of her lips. They kissed again, and yet again; and the burden of the future rolled away from him, and he knew that it did not matter, after all, if after to-night he never saw her, if he never even learnt her name. He had got something that could not be taken away from him; and he was willing, now, to pay for it with heartache.

No words were exchanged. They did not speak until they were near the house, on the broad gravel path below Claribel's balcony. In Claribel's studio the lights were burning, but only the top of the uncurtained windows was visible, and one could not see inside.

'What's that?' said Sylens suddenly. Something gleamed before them, on the ground beside the path.

Theresa picked it up. 'It's my sister's,' she said, looking at it curiously. 'I wonder how she came to lose it here.' She handed it to Sylens, holding it by the point, so that the hilt was towards him. 'Will you take care of it for the present? I have nowhere to keep it just now.'

He took it from her, looking not at it but at her. She was smiling; and he was aware that her gesture had significance. Still wondering, he slipped it, point uppermost, into an inner breast-pocket. Something in her tone had made it clear that she wished him to keep it hidden. Was she giving it to him? But it was not hers.

'Perhaps by now your sister will have missed it,' he said tentatively.

'Perhaps,' said Theresa. 'We shall see.'

'If she has, am I to return it?'

'I leave that,' said Theresa, 'to you.'

'But I can't keep what isn't mine!'

Theresa looked at him, faintly smiling. 'You *can*,' she said, 'if you have the courage. It takes courage to steal things, you know. But I don't suppose you'll want to keep it, when you've looked at it.' Sylens put his hand to his inner pocket. 'No,' said Theresa, 'not here. Someone may come; and besides, it's too dark... Look after it for this evening, and give it to her when she goes. She is so careless, she deserves to be a little punished,' she laughed. 'It's so funny that after all it should come to you.'

'I don't see why,' he said. He hated her to have some secret source of amusement that he was not permitted to share.

'Ask *her*,' said Theresa.

Sylens said stubbornly, 'I shall give it back to no one but you. I don't know your sisters. I am not supposed to know to which of them this thing belongs.'

Theresa laid her hand on his arm. 'Don't be angry,' she murmured. 'Actually, it is better where it is, with you, than with any of us. And if you choose to keep it, I shan't give you away. It would be appropriate.' She added in a hurried whisper, 'I shall remember you always.'

Sylens walked away, back into the garden. In the light that fell from Claribel's window he turned the silver dagger over and over on his hand. And then, on the blade, he saw the name, and beside it the coat of arms. He drew his breath in sharply: this dagger, it seemed, could stab the soul...

As he came up the stairs, he passed Marcus, coming down. But they were both preoccupied, and hardly saw each other.

## 21

And now, they were all assembled in the upstairs room. Down the length of it ran tables set together to form one long board, which was laden with cakes and sandwiches and sweetmeats; but the guests did not sit round it. They sat back, in the shadows, along the walls. Gilbert had lighted all the candles of the Christmas tree. Champagne went round. And yet there was no air of festivity, no laughter, no loud exchange of words across the room. Conversation never rose above a murmur; and when it began, it quickly died away again. It was as if the thoughts of everyone present were concentrated on something else that was happening, or about to happen, in their midst. They waited, as at a solemn ceremony, a Mystery or a Mass, for something to be revealed; and meanwhile they took stock of their own thoughts.

The quiet, the absence of hilarity, would have seemed strange in any other company. But here everybody accepted it as natural, because it arose, not from indifference or boredom, but from the intensity of their interest. They felt as though they had been together for so long, in intimate contact, that they could not imagine the breaking-up of this society. The evening seemed like a lifetime – but no one present wished it to end. This was the only thought that they had in common; but it was sufficient to weld them together.

Claribel was the only one who seemed to have no preoccupation. She flitted about from the table to her guests, and Gilbert, a tall thin shadow, followed her. Her movements wove them together, and as she came and went, they watched her, as one watches the only animated object in an environment of stillness: a butterfly among flowers, or a bird among foliage. She had changed her costume again, and wore a white silk shirt and navy blue trousers, with a short cloak thrown over her shoulders. Markakis, watching her, thought that at least she had a certain style, that one might call beauty in one's more hypnotized moments. And above all, she had variety: she did provide entertainment... He got up and went to the piano, and began to play, this time of Claribel. Not *for* her; he had long since passed that folly. He felt lighthearted, and he played a gay, rippling tune. A burden had rolled from him: he was, he believed, heart-whole at last, alone. No friend: Claribel had freed him from friendship. No mistress: the three sisters, by their mere presence, had cured him of even that desire. No dependence on anyone for approval, or even for a hearing: henceforward, his own sure touch on the instrument, as he talked to himself in sound, would be enough. No more books: he would pursue his own imaginings, his own lovely memories, so elusive, so enchanting, down the labyrinthine corridors of his own mind.

He played; and now, it was all different. Nobody had asked him; he did not need to be asked. But nobody would stop him, either; they no longer wished to. His playing mingled with their own thoughts. *They* had no need to listen, that was why they showed no resistance. Before, they had shut their ears to what he was saying; and as soon as they had dared, they had talked. It had been almost as if they had wished to shout him down. But now, his music insinuated itself without their noticing; it wove them together, as Claribel herself was doing, and brightened their expectancy. He was masterful now, like Marcus: no longer their slave. The dark eyed princess with the smooth dark hair, the white forehead and the delicate nose – she had been his salvation. But she was too remote to trouble his peace – as remote as the slender Minoan ladies on the frescoes of his home. It was good that she had fallen to the lot of Marcus; he was worthy of her...

Imperceptibly his music changed: the rippling, superficial melody had given way to a larger, more serious air that was the theme of the princess, and through that there broke on his own startled ears an heroic, sword-like phrase that stood for Marcus. He united them, severed them, and after many wandering variations, united them again. Claribel's tune had vanished altogether: she was forgotten in a solemn, triumphal march in which Marcus and the princess paced together... How well matched they were! Marcus had always been wasted on Claribel. Still, one must not be hard on Claribel: she was what she was, and that at least was not the boring convention of consistency so dear to most Saxon women. And so, by being herself, vain and shallow and changeable, she achieved a reality that was more interesting than a sham ideal. And she did more good than she knew, or even got credit for doing: for she released others from their sham selves, so that they did not need to feel too deeply or think too highly of her. She set them free in the long run, free even to hate her if they pleased.

He wondered if Marcus and the Princess Lucy were listening: if they understood his music. Music was wonderful; one could say everything in fullest, rounded, completest candour, and no one knew. What a fool he had been ever to complain of not being understood. If he had said in words what he was now playing to them, the whole company would have been aghast; there would have been shame, embarrassment, feuds; an immediate combination of them against him, the speaker, the teller of truth; a stopping of him at all costs. Music is the only truthful art, for music alone is free to speak truth in a world that cannot tolerate the smallest morsel of it. It has a very weak stomach, our society! Markakis laughed inside. Here he sat, playing the whole thing to them, all that he had seen and heard; and they listened, it went into them, and remained uninterpreted, like the Minoan clay tablets, or the hieroglyphics before they found the Rosetta stone! Heaven forbid that there should ever be a Rosetta stone for music! Luckily, this was impossible. But the miracle of music was more wonderful than that of any script unread. The lines on the tablets meant nothing to the onlooker; without the clue they were scratches of tantalizing design. But music, never understood, yet found its way into the soul, and had its effect. Marcus and the princess would never say to him, 'You know our secret. We heard you repeat it to this company'; but when his tune was played, they would be a little different, more intent. Something would have been shown to them, crystallized for them, so that they could never forget it, or lose grip of the purpose that carried them towards that end.

So Markakis, with his back to the company, played on, of that scene in the garden, when standing in the shadow of the house he had watched Marcus and Lucy take leave of each other, and Lucy had given him the shining dagger; of the light in Claribel's studio, and the voices, and how the dagger had come hurtling through the window into the border beside the path. Markakis had wondered if he should go and get it, and give it back to one or other of them. Which? On whose side was he? On *what* side was he, harmony or discord? Should he give it back to Marcus, and let all be as it was before? That seemed too tame, and not quite fair to Claribel, to let her rather brave effort come to nothing. Should he give it back to Lucy and raise the storm? It would be grand to see Lucy angry. But then, she might be so angry that she would merely keep the dagger and not deign even to tell Marcus that it had come back to her. That too would be a waste. It would also be playing into the hands of Claribel, who did not deserve such chance assistance.

He could, of course, keep it himself, and get them all on a string. Claribel would do a lot to get it back; so would Marcus. Lucy – no, one could not play with her. But one could perhaps do her a service, or let her think so; and earn her gratitude. One would have to be careful, though, there: she was not to be easily deceived. The other two – well, he could decide later.

He was just about to come out of his hiding-place and take the dagger, when he heard voices; and Theresa and Sylens came out of the wood...

Oh, wonderful to look at Claribel, to look at Lucy, to look at Marcus, and know that each was thinking about the same thing; to know what that thing was, and where it was. What wouldn't each of them have given to have his knowledge! One could, if one knew, actually see the outline of die dagger under Sylens' coat on the left side! One could run one's finger along it in front of them, and still they wouldn't see. Sylens too would be startled, if his possession were revealed. What would he do with it? He was the man to watch now. This was far better, even than holding the dagger in one's own keeping; for one need take no difficult decision, one had only to watch.

A marvellous game for a New Year's Eve party; and all his own. Markakis played on without looking round.

## 22

Marcus sat back in the shadows looking on.

Claribel had failed to find the dagger: now what was the next step? It was not his custom to be put out by a reverse; his mind went on quietly functioning, no matter how tricky the job, nor how short the time in which to do it. And Marcus cared deeply that over this trifle he should not be defeated. It offended his pride that he should make such a mess of anything, however small. Was it small? The loss of the dagger was not, looked at *sub specie aeternitatis*, a disaster. But to Lucy it would be a matter of some importance, else she would not have chosen to give it to him. He had not looked at it closely, but in those few moments of holding it in his hand, he had realized that it was valuable, intrinsically. As for its real value, to her, that was clearly beyond estimate.

And she had handed it to him on an impulse: and impulses, he knew, were rare with her. It was to be the magic clue by which he was to find her again, and he had lost it, like a fool, within a few minutes of receiving it! He had been so sure of having plenty of time that he had not even taken the trouble to examine it, to find out what mark it bore by which he should know who its owner was. He had, tamely, with incredible weakness, allowed the other woman to put her hand in his pocket and rob him of his treasure! What was the matter with him? Was he a man no longer? Had contact with that blonde baby really softened his sinews, his morale, to such an extent that he could behave like a fascinated rabbit in an emergency? He had prided himself on his ability to react quickly. And see, when for once it had really mattered, he had ignominiously failed. Even Gilbert was not such a sap as he, Marcus, had proved himself to be.

He looked down the room to where the three sisters sat, reunited. That was how he liked to see them: grouped together, Ursula in a high-backed chair, Lucy beside her in a slightly lower chair, Theresa on a footstool at their feet. They must have sat thus for many a portrait. He saw the three profiles outlined against the fire. Yes, Theresa was the most beautiful, Ursula the wisest; why did he so greatly prefer Lucy? Why was it that her form, smaller than theirs, her slanting profile, really very much like theirs and yet to him utterly different, filled him with an emotion for which he could find no better name than – satisfaction, the pleasure one gets from seeing something really good at last? He did not know whether or not it should be called love: it seemed to him sometimes that he was no longer capable of that, if indeed he ever had been. At any rate, he had spent himself for so long on a fake that he seemed to have no response of passion left for the real. No, his concern was due not so much to the fact that he still did not know her name or where to find her; he was not sure whether, even if he still had the dagger, he would follow her and risk that second meeting. He was sure that if he listened to wisdom, he would not go; and it was no longer certain that he would not listen to wisdom. What troubled him, what made the back of his neck grow red with shame, was his own bungling; for unless he recovered the dagger, he would have to tell her. It would be hateful to have to confess; but better confession even, than that she should think, if she never saw him again, his not coming was due to lack of enterprise or lack of desire, when it was due to impotence.

Marcus watched her and let the music ripple over him, and thought…

Claribel came towards him; she looked charming in her white shirt, and her short cloak thrown back to show the scarlet lining, and caught by a silver chain round her throat. Charming, but as uninteresting, to him, as a china doll. She was a stranger. Her round white arms were bare; she held out plates of food towards him, leaning forward with a slightly supplicatory gesture. He noticed everything about her, that had – it seemed so very long ago – appealed to his senses and titillated his mind. Yet she was a stranger, except in so far as she could help him to get back what she had caused him to lose. That was her only interest for him. The past twelve years had not created one single bond between them; and when he left her to-night, he believed that even her physical appearance would fade from his memory. Time has nothing to do with the depth of impressions; there was many a face seen only once, perhaps in a shop or in the street, that would come back to him, uncalled for, in odd moments of dreaming; but Claribel's – the time would come when he would fail to evoke it, even if he tried to do so; when he *would*, try, for curiosity's sake, and would achieve separate features, but not the whole. This had happened to him already, sometimes, when he had been far away and had wished to be sentimental; but he had refused to heed the obvious implication...

He took a sandwich from the dish. She leaned closer. The only person near them was Markakis, on the other side of the grand piano, and he was absorbed in his music. Still, it was better to speak enigmatically than to whisper. Markakis, even if he heard, would not be able to interpret.

'Did you solve the mystery?' he said, as though indifferently.

Claribel leaned forward and whispered. 'It was not there. Someone must have picked it up. Someone in this room.' She glanced back furtively. 'They were all out in the garden. No one from outside could have got so close to the house without being seen.'

'No, so I thought,' said Marcus. And he went on in his normal voice, taking no notice of her eyes that were fixed on him eagerly, 'You must do something about it, you know.'

'What *can* I do?' whispered Claribel. 'I can't *ask*. Even you wouldn't want me to do that, I suppose.'

'No,' said Marcus, 'no.' He thought for a moment, and then said, 'I wonder if the finder was a man or a woman. If it were a man, one could perhaps find out...'

'How?' said Claribel, hanging on his words.

Marcus lowered his voice. 'There is dancing. Whoever found it must surely have it on his or her person.'

'I don't know. Whoever found it must have wanted to hide it, or they would have mentioned it. Unless, of course, they knew the owner, and returned it direct.' Her eyes glittered spitefully.

'I had wondered that,' said Marcus. 'I must investigate that possibility also. Meanwhile, I leave you to deal with the men.'

'That's not much good,' said Claribel. 'Suppose whoever has it doesn't choose to dance, or doesn't dance with *me*.'

'You're right,' said Marcus. He thought again. 'Your game before supper was popular, wasn't it? Well, we must play it again. You must announce it. First a little dancing perhaps, and then, more murder-party. They will agree if you speak convincingly. People can't have too much of a good thing. Then – the rest is up to you and me. But,' he continued coolly, 'if you fail, Claribel, God help you. And remember, the time is short.'

Claribel bit her lip. 'Be damned to you,' she said. 'I shan't bother myself. Why should I? What makes you think I'm such a fool as to exert myself over your new flame? If you must know, I'm glad the thing is lost, and I shan't lift a finger to help you find it—'

Marcus rose.

'Just a minute, everybody,' he said. 'Excuse me, Markakis. Claribel wants to know what we're going to do next. She was wondering if you'd like a change – charades or something. We can, of course, have some more murder-party – that's what I suggested – but Claribel thinks you'll be bored–'

He was interrupted by applause and denials. They all wanted to go on playing the dangerous and progressively more exciting game.

'A little dancing first, then,' said Marcus. He could never resist postponing the best till the end. He liked also to toy with danger. 'Sure nobody would like to join Claribel in charades?'

The guests murmured. It was clear they didn't want to. Marcus smiled benignly down on Claribel. She, with her back still to the room, threw at him a look of answering spite, then turned and smiled dazzlingly at the others.

Markakis also was smiling as he rounded off his performance with a few triumphant chords.

## 23

The three sisters sat together at their end of the room, not talking, surveying the scene. Ursula was in a dream, wondering why she had encouraged John Carraway, when in an hour's time she would be gone, inevitably, and for ever; or rather, Carraway himself and all that she saw before her would have vanished like a mirage, and she be left standing, cold and alone, herself again. For a little while, charmed by Carraway's own words and the strange atmosphere that surrounded her, she had allowed herself to believe in the mirage; but unlike him, she was no romantic at heart; and the spell was breaking. Already she could feel it. Something had touched her – some cold breath from the world of reality had impinged, and she was aware of a change of mood. She would not, if she could help it, talk with Carraway again: not because she was afraid – that was over – but because she knew that he could not prevail; and she wished to be spared the spectacle of his failure. She dreamed on, happy in the sight of her sisters' smooth heads, the dark and the fair, below her, within reach of her hand. She was not sad at all.

Lucy, too, was dreaming.

Her eyes rested on Claribel, talking to Marcus at the other end of the room; but she was not thinking of them. She was not even wondering what Claribel, standing over him and leaning towards him so confidentially, could be saying. Claribel and her relationship with Marcus did not interest her. What she wondered was, how he would deal with the clue she had given him. Would it lead him back to her some day? And if he came, would she then be willing to receive him? Or would it seem, by that time, a tiresome mistake, best forgotten? She did not so far regret her impulse; she felt safe, secure, as she rested her arm on Ursula's knee, and felt the pressure of Theresa's young, thin shoulder-blades against her own knees. She could not believe that Marcus would ever achieve an entry into her charmed circle, into which she would withdraw the moment he, or anyone else alarming, threatening to her personality, came too near. Yet how disappointed she would be, how flat and stale the future would instantly become, if she were sure that she had nothing to fear from him! She did fear him: that is to say, she feared lest he could and would break down barriers. There was not about him the faintest suggestion of cruelty, but he had a quality with which cruelty is often con-fused – ruthlessness, a relentless pursuit of a given end. If he hurt, it would never be for the sake of hurting – that is cruelty; but he would hurt, even kill, incidentally, and either not notice it, or not care...

She gave a low laugh, and threw back her dark head, so that the ends of her hair brushed Ursula's knee.

'You know,' she said, in an ordinary tone, but more quietly, 'just now, I gave away my dagger to that man at the end of the room there.'

There was a pause. Theresa did not turn round. Ursula said:

'Yes, dear, you told me so. But were you wise?'

'Wise? I don't know. That is what I hope to find out.'

'You are not sorry yet?'

'No. I am sure I shall see it again one day. I am wondering when and where.'

Theresa turned her profile towards them.

'You were silly,' she said calmly, 'to trust that large man. He looks reliable, but it is a sham. He has lost your dagger, Lucy, already.'

Lucy did not stir. She said coldly, 'How do you know?'

'Because it was I who found it, lying in the garden where he had let it fall. I thought it was you who had lost it, and I wondered when you would find out it was gone.'

'Then you have it now? Give it to me.' Lucy's face was composed, though pale, and her satin slipper tapped the ground. Theresa smiled and shook her head.

'No, I gave it to my poet. Don't be afraid, *he* won't lose it, he is more reliable than your explorer. He is carrying it next to his heart. I can almost see it, inside his coat. Look, and you will see its outline.'

'Go at once and get it from him,' said Lucy, sternly. 'It was not yours to give.'

'No?' said Theresa, unperturbed. 'But it was mine to lend, because I found it. I don't know yet whether he has had time to look at it, but I wished him to...'

'Go at once and ask him for it,' repeated Lucy, 'or I will.'

Ursula added gently, 'You must go, Theresa.'

Theresa rose and crossed towards Sylens. He stood up as she approached him. It was just as they were about to meet that Marcus broke off his conversation with Claribel, and claimed the attention of the room.

'Just a minute, everybody —' Markakis stopped playing. Everyone turned to hear. Theresa, interested, forgot her errand. When Marcus had gained his point, and she was about to turn to Sylens she found Lucy beside her.

'Say nothing, Theresa,' said Lucy. 'I have changed my mind.'

Theresa turned to her in surprise. Lucy stopped her question impatiently.

'Do as I ask. I mean what I say. I have decided,' – and the flicker of a smile crossed her lips – 'to give my explorer a chance of retrieving his error. It will be more interesting that way.'

The two sisters returned, arm in arm, to Ursula. Sylens stared after them, amazed.

## 24

They were downstairs again, dancing.

Markakis was no longer needed to put on the gramophone records: by now there was better dance music being broadcast, and Dione's portable wireless set, looking expensive in its tan leather case, was making even Markakis' presence unnecessary. Claribel was not there either, nor Gilbert: presumably they were dismantling the table in the room above. The dancers felt at their ease, and they chose the partners they wanted, and stayed with them, now that there was no bright hostess, no host with a sense of duty, to thread a way between them and break up, in the interests of sociability, a too-long-standing combination. For the trouble about modern dancing is that it readily becomes a tête-à-tête; and Claribel and Gilbert tried always to guard against this at their parties.

And so, through waltz and tango and slow-fox, Carraway held Ursula in his arms, and Marcus held Lucy, and Peggy had at last got hold of Desmond, and even Betty had managed to capture and keep with her a tall, sinister-looking Irishman, who seemed to get a dark and secret pleasure out of her rigid dancing and thin, virginal form. He did not speak a word to her; he clasped her very tightly with his bony arm, and stared out across her blonde head with a look of grim intentness. Even when the dances changed, he scarcely relaxed his grip; and the moment the band struck up, he grabbed her to him and began again. She was in a trance of happiness, though she did not really like him and was a little uncomfortable. Her neck ached with the effort to prevent her face from being crushed against his dark, prickly jaw; she would have liked the sensation, but her upbringing impelled her to resist it as far as was in her power. However, the choice was not always left to her, so that when the unavoidable contact occurred, she could resign herself to it without any naggings of conscience to spoil it. What should a well-brought-up girl do in such circumstances? Should she disengage herself? The rough man would not have allowed it; and if she had struggled or protested, how these hateful, over-sophisticated people would have laughed at her! Even the elegant sisters would have smiled. It was more dignified to pretend that nothing unusual was happening; and oh, in spite of alarm how much better it was than sitting alone by the fire! Now, she would be able to hold her own with Peggy, when they went home together: otherwise Peggy would have been insufferable now that she too was succeeding. The Irishman danced very badly; he trod on her feet with his clumsy shoes. There was not a man in the room with whom she would not rather be dancing. Marcus, for instance... but he was wholly absorbed.

Yes, during this long evening, Betty had had time to look round her; and her fancy had pitched on Marcus. She had been watching him. She loved his great size, his plain red face, the fact that he wore tweeds and clumsy shoes – like her partner, but in Marcus it somehow became fascinating, as it was desirable that he should step on her toes. She had conceived a passion for him, a passion which she freely admitted to herself, and gloated over, but which she would never confess to anyone else. It filled her with shame; it was outrageous, because it was hopeless, but it burnt within her like a many-coloured flame, and she would not have quenched it if she had been able. She thought him magnificent, grand; she coveted him, and yet if – as at times she half expected he would – if he had become aware of the pressure of her interest upon him, and been drawn towards her, she would have wanted to run away and hide. But she knew, actually, that this would not be: love had given her perception, and she knew that, so long as Lucy was there, he was immune, insulated from all other contacts. And such is the power of love upon even the shallow and the vain, that she did not altogether wish anything to be altered; she was filled with the terrible longing for self-sacrifice that may descend upon those most conscious of, and intent on, their little dues, and if he wanted to be with Lucy, she wished it also. Moreover, she could feel a transferred emotion, puzzled, diffident, slightly angry, towards Lucy herself: if Marcus admired her, she did too. But neither of them cared; there is nothing more baffling than to be visited by an emotion which can have no expression because it has not, and never can have, the slightest interest for its object.

Every time that they passed her in the dance she writhed slightly in the Irishman's grip, and turned her neck sufficiently to be able to see them, though she knew that she would have to pay for this each time by a tightening of his embrace, if that was possible. Well, she could enjoy that too. Recklessness, foreign to her cautious, calculating little soul, possessed her, because of Marcus. She responded to her partner's pressure by a barely perceptible movement, a relaxation of muscles that had been held rigid before; and instantly he thought how true it was that there is no girl, however virginal she looks, who doesn't want to be seduced, when the idea is put to her. He flattered himself that he was putting it very clearly; and if later on she pretended she hadn't understood, he would undoubtedly register it as another example of women's incorrigible hypocrisy.

Betty was thinking, 'How I loathe this creature!' But she went on, encouraging him in her prim way, as well as she knew how; for it seemed to make her more worthy of Marcus that someone, even this satyr, should want to dance with her, and should trouble to treat her as if she were a woman, instead of a sexless schoolgirl. Afterwards she would let the satyr take her outside and kiss her if he wanted to; and she would feel terribly lost and abandoned, while Marcus, only a few yards away behind the wall, talked gravely to his new friend, and Lucy as gravely listened, looking down.

'I love you,' crooned the wireless, 'with such a tender passion...' At that moment Marcus and Lucy passed them; the picture they made was stamped on Betty's over-excited brain. A change had come over them, invisible to others, terribly clear to her. In Marcus it was not so great: he still looked, as always, composed, sure of himself, imperturbable; he still held his partner loosely, a little distance away, and he danced nonchalantly, as one who had been brought up to do the polka and the barn-dance, and wasn't sufficiently exercised by these modern walking dances. Anyone not in love with him might have thought him somewhat awkward. But Betty did not: he was different from the other men, cleaner and finer, because he did not turn dancing into a sexual orgy. Yet in spite of his composure, she saw in his face and bearing something that had not been there when first, at the beginning of this very evening – how long ago! – she had seen him, after he had leaned forward and laid his big red hand upon Peggy's shoulder. There had gone from it all that expression of – not exactly tiredness; he was too strong for that – but endurance, as though a weight were pressing on his shoulders, against which he had to brace the whole of his great strength in order to remain so magnificently upright, as he succeeded in doing. Now all that was gone; the weight was lifted, or had rolled away, and his bearing was free and young again. His look was more than composed, it was serene.

And Lucy? In her the change was startling. It would pass when this dance, this unique dance, with Claribel away, in which all were themselves, was ended. Betty felt that she ought not to look on; for Lucy was unaware that she was being observed, or even that there was anything for an observer to see. Nor was there, except for preternaturally sharpened vision; but to Betty it was a revelation of Lucy's soul. Lucy's dark head was flung back, so that her smooth hair fell in heavy waves on each side of her pale face. But it was not only her pallor that was noticeable, nor the redness of her slightly parted lips. It was the air of abandon to an intense inner conflict, from which one would gladly rest but cannot: as of someone who fights a battle which he cannot win, and will not lose. Betty, in her strange clairvoyance, seemed to know what that conflict was, and why it was draining the strength of its victim: why Marcus seemed to glow with the youth he had lost, and Lucy for the moment looked years older than her age. 'She will give in,' thought Betty, and a spasm of hate contracted her heart. But she would not have had it otherwise; indeed, if she had had the chance, she would have added her persuasions. It was not only that if Marcus wanted anything she wished him to have it; it was that she thought Lucy worthy of him. And this was not only because she admired Lucy, but because she detested Claribel.

Nobody knew with what furious hatred she regarded Claribel. She had concealed it from everyone; from her family, from Peggy, even from herself. Claribel flattered her, called her beautiful, sketched her, and now had asked her to this party. But it had all been done in such a way that Betty was made to realize, deeply and painfully, her shortcomings. Always, with Claribel, she felt herself to be a thin, awkward schoolgirl, whom Claribel sketched, not for the reasons she alleged, but because she saw in Betty a type, curious but not so very rare: the thin virgin who now, at seventeen, possessed an austere charm due solely to the bloom of youth; who must therefore quickly be seized and conveyed to papers and canvas, because that bloom would fade as quickly as the glow of sunrise, and leave behind mere angularity, a hard outline than which nothing could be less attractive. Betty felt that, even when sketching her, Claribel was forecasting her future, and somehow helping to bring it about.

Betty had always felt embarrassed, ill at ease, in Claribel's society; but she had not realized how active was her hatred until she heard Peggy's tale of Claribel's lovers, and that Marcus was one of them. It was this that had drawn her attention to Marcus, and then to his companion. She rejoiced, therefore, when she saw them more and more together. Claribel had lost him: this was all that mattered. And if Claribel tried to interfere, tried to get him back again, as Betty was sure she would, she, Betty, would be prepared to murder her. She thought of her thin fingers closing on Claribel's soft round throat, tighter and tighter... But that was nonsense. There was one person in whose interest it was to restrain Claribel, and that was he whom everyone discounted – Gilbert, her husband. Betty, when she had heard from Peggy's lips the story of Gilbert's complacency, of his withdrawal in favour of Marcus, had been appalled. She felt herself profoundly shocked, morally outraged; she did not know that, besides the unfamiliarity of the idea and its antagonism to all she had been taught, there was in her moral indignation the resentment that everything should be made so easy for Claribel. She had felt, then, an itch that Gilbert should have his eyes opened to his position, how absurd it was, how undignified and unseemly. If it would have been of any use, she would have almost been prepared to remonstrate with him... Betty was one of nature's busybodies; at forty she would have blossomed into some species of reformer, probably a social worker, and undoubtedly a most unpleasant neighbour.

Her brain was on fire. Love for Marcus, romantic interest in Lucy, hatred of Claribel, had worked on her imagination so that facts no longer mattered. She did not stop to remember that she did not know more than a fragment of the truth; the picture for her was complete: Marcus and Lucy, ideally suited to each other, but certain to be thwarted by the diabolical Claribel, while Gilbert, unaware that the moment for action had come, weakly stood by and did nothing to prevent the mischief. Perhaps the unaccustomed wine, and the bold overtures of her partner, had helped to confuse her. At any rate she suddenly saw herself in the role of guardian angel to that heroic, star-crossed pair: she said to the Irishman, 'Let me go,' so abruptly and with such a determined twist of her thin young body, that before he was aware of it, he had released her. Her face had gone thin and sharp; he looked at her in amazement, and at a loss. This was no girlish caprice: she meant it. She did not wish to be recaptured or even pursued. And as always happens when one means what one says, she got her way. She turned and pushed through the crowded, rhythmically rocking circle of dancers to the door. A minute before and the man would have followed her; but even he was aware that there was no invitation in her movement, merely a purpose in which he had no share. He shrugged his shoulders, therefore, and went to the sideboard to get a drink.

Betty, like one hypnotized, closed the door, and began to mount the stairs.

## 25

Lucy said, as she danced with Marcus: 'I know you have lost my dagger.'

'Do you?' he said imperturbably. He no longer cared. While she was with him, and he could talk to her, the affair of the dagger seemed trivial, a childish game. Unless, of course, she regarded it as symbolic.

'You lost it very quickly,' she said.

'Yes. I was unlucky. Or rather, I was off my guard. One is, you know, at a party. You must not treat it as an indication of character.'

'I don't. Not in the sense you mean. But the dagger is – valuable.'

'I shall replace it,' he said.

'You couldn't. It is very old – an heirloom.'

'Not so old,' said Marcus, 'as the one I shall give you. You shall choose the pick of my collection – Greek, Egyptian, Sumerian, what you will.'

There was a pause. 'What assurance you have!' she said. 'I don't believe you are even worried that you have lost my dagger. Well, I expect you *have* better ones – more valuable in themselves, or even to me. But not more valuable to you, perhaps.'

'Why not?' said Marcus, interested.

'Because my name is written on the handle, and unless you know that, you won't be able to find me. I flattered myself, I see, in thinking that that would make you keep it carefully.'

'Claribel knows your name,' said Marcus. 'She will tell it me.'

'No,' said Lucy, sombrely, 'Claribel will not tell it to you.'

'Oh yes, she will,' smiled Marcus. 'She promised me a surprise after you had gone. She intends to tell me. If she changes her mind, I will make her.'

'Claribel will never tell you,' repeated Lucy, 'neither you nor anyone else. She is under oath not to do so.'

Marcus laughed. 'You think that will prevent her? But what does it matter? I shall find out, if not through her, then in some other way. To begin with, before this night is over, I shall recover the dagger.'

Lucy flashed up a look at him. His confidence was superb.

'I hope you will,' she said, 'for I warn you, if I get it first – and I intend to try – we shall never meet again.'

'Then that makes it imperative,' said Marcus.

'You have only a very little time. Soon after midnight we shall be gone.' She looked up again to see if she had shaken his calm, but he was still smiling. 'And what is more, I know where it is.'

Marcus' expression did not change. 'Of course you do,' he said. 'So do I, now... You have a great advantage in that there are *three* of you. And yet you haven't made use of your knowledge. And so I imagine you are leaving it to me. You see, I was watching that little exchange upstairs just now.'

'I had only to ask for it –'

'But you didn't. And you won't.'

'No. But short of that –' She shook his arm impatiently. 'Why don't you stop dancing with me, and make a start?'

'I prefer to be with you,' said Marcus, 'since the time is so short; and also I prefer to keep you with me.'

He meant the remark playfully. He did not know how it sounded to Lucy's ears.

## 26

As they danced, Carraway was saying to Ursula:
'You aristocrats are all barbarians at heart. You are a racial experiment. The world keeps certain families, noble or royal, just as a rich man keeps peacocks or prize horses. You are preserved and pampered, given every luxury, every advantage of culture. In return, it is asked of you that you allow yourselves on occasion to be stared at and admired. You are an experiment in breeding the perfect human animal.'

'Some of us,' said Ursula, 'have been asked to *rule*.'

'Yes – but how badly you have done it! Still, the amazing thing is you have done it no worse. It was too much to expect of anything so ill understood as heredity, that it should provide us with a string of even moderately competent rulers. A great monarch has a son: to expect him to inherit his father's or mother's genius is idiotic; the utmost that can happen is that, brought up from childhood in the atmosphere, he may assimilate enough knowledge of the craft to amount to adequacy in office, just as the son of a doctor has, I suppose, less difficulty in mugging up the facts of medicine than the son of a bartender. But genius! The history of the arts should teach you better than that. I tell you, human progress depends on individuals, not on dynasties.'

He was flushed, and he had forgotten that he danced rather badly. He was really angry with Ursula; at the moment, she stood for all he hated.

'You talk like an artist,' she said contemptuously.

'I am proud to hear you say so.'

'A painter of trees.'

'Yes. A tree has no nationality. Take a German tree and plant it in France, and it grows just as well, provided the soil and the climate are right. Trees observe natural laws, they do not erect artificial barriers and then murder each other in defence of them or in a passion to extend them. You would die for your country. I don't know what your country is, but I gather it is one of those that feels itself oppressed. What is worse, you would kill for your country. In fact, there is no crime you wouldn't think it right to commit in your country's name. You would employ all your talents, all the learning you have had the luck to acquire, you would sell your freedom, your right to choose a husband, your children's future, all in defence of a system that is doomed – doomed, I tell you, and rightly so. You would like to produce a Frederick the Great, to lead another Thirty Years' War, and tear Europe asunder with hate and fear again. And your sisters? Are they of the same mind?'

'We think and feel as one,' said Ursula.

'How horrible!' said Carraway with violence.

Ursula said calmly: 'You think differently. I shall tell you why. Because you belong to a great, rich, powerful country, in which there is no longer any need for every able-bodied man and woman to work for its preservation. Other men have done that for you; they do it still, on the outskirts, but you are unaware. You live inside the circle of their protection. Shall I tell you why my country's art is inferior to yours? Because we have never had time to devote ourselves to amusement. We have no outstandingly great painter, or poet, or musician: we have our folk-songs, our folk-dances, our pageantry. Your country can afford to keep a few hundreds of the idle and irresponsible to entertain it – just as it can afford to maintain its lunatics in luxurious asylums in order to enjoy the sensation of being humane. In my country, each family has to look after its own sick and aged and insane.'

Carraway said: 'An hour ago, I thought I was in love with you – that I should like to marry you.'

Ursula laughed. 'I know you did. I didn't want to offend you, because as a man you are charming. But –'

'Not cut out to be the father of a Frederick the Great,' sneered Carraway.

'No,' said Ursula blandly. 'And heaven knows, I'm not cut out to be the mother of a painter of trees.'

'Still, I shall always regret you – that with all your gifts and all your beauty, you had a barbarian soul.'

'And I shall regret you – that with all your intelligence and insight, you have the mind of a child.'

'You understand nothing,' said Carraway sadly. 'Oh, if I could teach you to see life as a whole!'

Ursula smiled. 'You *see* nothing,' she said, 'not even what is going on within the four walls of this room, much less outside them.'

Something in her tone startled Carraway. He stopped dancing and looked at her. 'What do you mean?' he said. 'That reminds me: I have meant to ask you all along, why did you come here? Aren't you wasting your time, mixing with all these childish and irresponsible people? I wonder what you are doing in England at all. *Who are you*, Ursula? Won't you tell me that, just before you go?'

Ursula shook her head. 'There will be no need. You will discover.'

'How? By asking Claribel?'

'There will be no need for that either. But you can find out from her if you stay on at the party. She is going to tell all her guests, I believe. We wish that this could be prevented, but it is, I'm afraid, impossible.'

'Yes. One should never entrust a secret to Claribel. She is completely untrustworthy. So long as one knows that about her –'

'We have discovered it,' said Ursula, 'and of course, taken it into account when making our plans. I am sure our hostess won't give us away until we are gone.'

Somewhat to Carraway's surprise, she turned away and left him. He saw her speak, in passing, first to Lucy, then to Theresa. Lucy shook her head in answer. Theresa nodded and smiled.

## 27

Theresa, as soon as they began dancing, said to Sylens:

'You know, you will have to look after the dagger carefully. That man dancing with my sister – he will be trying to get it back again. It was he who lost it she gave it him to carry. And he dropped it.'

'That wasn't like Marcus,' said Sylens.

'No? Well, nobody is being like themselves this evening, do you think? Anyway, she knows where it is.'

'You told her?'

'Oh, yes, I couldn't resist it. She was angry! She sent me across to you to ask you for it – but then she changed her mind. I don't know why. I think she wants the explorer to prove he is not as stupid as he seems. But *I* want *you* to prove that a poet is as good as an explorer.'

'But the dagger is your sister's,' said Sylens. 'I can't keep it if she asks me for it.'

'But she won't,' said Theresa impatiently. 'Haven't I told you, she doesn't want to get it back that way? And so it will be a fight, and that will be fun. You see?'

'But,' Sylens objected again, 'Praed happens to be a friend of mine. I don't wish to compete with him. If your sister is making a kind of test match out of it, I don't wish to score at his expense.'

'Not even,' said Theresa, 'for me?'

'Not even for you.'

'I see. Your friend, who is here on the spot, is more to you than I, who am going away. I didn't think you were so – crude.'

Sylens was distressed, but obstinate. 'But, Theresa, it doesn't matter at all to you, does it, who has the dagger? It isn't as if it were yours, and I were keeping it for you. Why should *you* want to make a test match out of it? Your sister's attitude is just understandable. But yours is – pure caprice, and rather unkind.'

Theresa smiled up at him dazzlingly. 'Perhaps you are right. Forgive me. I didn't know he was your friend. I merely saw it as Lucy did – as a piece of fun. I was stupid. Let's forget about it and dance.'

They danced for some time without speaking. Sylens was troubled. He knew that in those few moments something had changed. He had not really gained his point. He had merely offended Theresa, and therefore he was to waste what little of the evening remained. After this evening he would never see her again. She would go back to her strange, remote life in that capital whose name was written on the dagger, the famous dagger that seemed to be causing so much discord. Even if he followed her, he could not know her in her own country. And even if, for this queer evening's sake, she consented, and was allowed to consent, to receive him, well, he would have half an hour's formal conversation with a stranger, and then he would pass on, feeling wretched, humiliated because nothing he could ever do or be would give him entry into her enchanted world. How ironical now seemed all his notions about living in the present, not bothering about the future! How she must have smiled, with what amused indulgence, when he had lectured her – as it now seemed to him – on seizing the moment! She had known all the time that he had no choice.

And now, he had lost even the moment. He had been, in his way, as clumsy as Marcus. He ought to have pretended to have played their game; it was stupid of him to have gone serious about it. As if it mattered! Marcus probably didn't care. Marcus was in the same position as himself, enjoying the society of a girl he would never see again after this evening, enjoying the piquancy of it, and possibly annoying Claribel. No one had seen Claribel for a long time. She was probably sulking... Why had she, who couldn't bear not to be the centre of attention all the time, invited the three sisters? Snobbism, he supposed. Afterwards she would brag that once they had attended a party of hers incognito. However, no one would believe her... How silly, vain and banal poor Claribel would seem after these exotic creatures! Life, democratic, realistic life with bacon for breakfast, and suburbia, and catching trains and having one's hair cut and reading the paper – how banal that too would seem, how desolatingly dull and vulgar! For in relation to daily life, Claribel with all her shortcomings had provided a touch of the bizarre and therefore of interest. That was how she had collected them all. And if Claribel, compared with the three sisters, was as mud to marble, what in God's name was there going to be worth living for? Even work –

Ursula passed them, walking slowly towards the door. She had ended her conversation with Carraway, and addressed a few words, in a language Sylens would not even have recognized but for the writing on the dagger, first to Lucy, and then to Theresa. Theresa smiled and nodded. Ursula passed on.

A moment later Theresa stopped suddenly to pick up something from the ground.

'Oh, my sister's powder-box!' she said. 'I must run after her. Will you come with me? I might get lost in this house – the corridors are so dark.'

'Couldn't I take it to her?' said Sylens doubtfully.

'No, no. Come with me.' She gave him another of her dazzling smiles; and yet, strangely, his heart was not elated as it had been in the garden when she had said to him: 'I shall remember you always.' It was as if that had been the moment of parting: this was a queer, unreal sequel that ought not to have been allowed to happen. And now: she was plainly calling him on, in a way that was supposed to be irresistible, but which left him doubtful and cold. But he could not show himself a prig for the second time so quickly. He followed, therefore.

Outside the door, as soon as it had closed upon him she again astonished him. He found her in his arms, and her hands drawing his head down to her lips, in a kiss far more passionate than that of the garden. And yet, though he could not help the shiver of pleasure that ran through him, it was a cold, forlorn, empty pleasure, as if one kissed the glass of a picture instead of the reality. At last she released him, and left him to follow her down the dark corridor.

They had not gone far when they met Ursula coming back. This time Theresa spoke to her in English.

'Here, darling, your powder-box. How careless you are. Hadn't you missed it? Go back again, stupid, and powder your nose!'

'What are you doing here, child?' said Ursula. Her tone was harsh, almost scolding. Sylens, deeply embarrassed, could almost feel her eyes upon him in the dark. 'Run back and finish the dance. We shan't be here much longer, you know.'

Theresa laughed shrilly, took Sylens' hand, and hurried him back along the corridor to the dance room again.

## 28

Gilbert and Markakis were left alone, in the upstairs room, to clear away the supper debris. Claribel, pleading other duties, had assigned this job to Gilbert, who accepted it without question, as he always did. But on her way out she had noticed Markakis, and it had occurred to her that he would no longer be needed downstairs to wind the gramophone, so she had asked him, very sweetly, if he would stay and help Gilbert. Markakis had agreed.

He was not being of much help, however. He leaned against the piano, watching Gilbert. Gilbert, silent, methodical and grave, was collecting remnants of food, stacking plates into piles, picking up discarded caps and cracker ends, restoring order. Even Gilbert did not seem to be as efficient as usual; his movements were continuous and regular, but they seemed slower, more automatic than purposive. He did not talk; he was wrapped up in himself, and appeared to be unaware of Markakis' presence. Markakis, with folded arms, watched him and smiled. At last he said harshly:

'It puzzles me.'

Gilbert looked up. His first look, when spoken to suddenly, was apt to seem hostile to those who did not know how mild and long-suffering he was. His dark complexion and hollow eyes were deceptive. Markakis went on:

'I've always wanted to ask you what you really thought about life. I mean, do you act as you do because you're indifferent, below par in your feelings; or is it deliberate, and are you out to break records, as it were, in self-effacement?'

Gilbert muttered something non-committal, and went on piling plates. One could not tell whether the conversation irritated or merely bored him. Markakis pursued:

'Claribel made you get the supper; and now she makes you clear it away. Doesn't it exasperate you sometimes to be pushed about according to her convenience? Especially as you don't get anything back at all. That's why I wanted to ask you, do you do it all deliberately, according to some scheme, or don't you mind?'

Gilbert put down the pile of plates he was carrying and came towards Markakis. 'I should advise you,' he said in his thin unpleasant voice, 'to mind your own business. You drank too much before supper, and you have been a nuisance all evening. If Claribel wishes, I shall throw you out.'

Markakis smiled. 'If Claribel wishes!' he sneered. 'I know what Claribel wishes, better than you do, it seems. She wants you to make yourself scarce while she tackles a little problem of her own. She wants me out of the way too, in case I should notice that she's not with her guests downstairs, and then I might get curious and start looking for her. She seems to suspect my good will towards her, I don't know why.'

But Gilbert's attention had been caught by one remark: he did not hear the rest. 'Not downstairs!' he said. 'How do you know? She is in her room then, or in the studio.'

'No, she isn't there either,' said Markakis, triumphantly. 'My dear fellow, I know a whole lot of things you don't, and by Father Zeus, I'm going to tell you them. Oh, don't withdraw. You simply mustn't, it's too good to be missed. It makes a story. That's why I'm telling you – because it makes such a damned good story that I *must* tell it to someone. It's all about a dagger, you know.'

'A dagger!' Gilbert stared at him amazed. He knew that Markakis was far gone in alcohol: at the stage before the final collapse, maybe, but at the moment he presented an appearance of godlike calm and omniscience.

'Yes, a dagger. The dagger belonging to the princess, the middle one, Lucy as she calls herself. And it is so damned funny; Claribel is out in the garden now, probably, looking for it. She doesn't believe anyone *can* have picked it up, and she's gone to have a last long look among the bushes... I wonder what she'd do if she found it. Would she give it back to Marcus? Why should she? Why should she help him with his lady friend? And yet probably that would be her best policy if she wants to keep him, because the princess will have gone by to-morrow, and there's really no hope for him there anyhow, so that if Claribel gave it back, she could get cheap gratitude and lose very little; but if Marcus doesn't get it back, he will certainly punish Claribel. So I think really she should try to help him, don't you?'

'What are you talking about?' said Gilbert. But his eyes were fixed on Markakis, and he was not missing a word.

'But what I can't make up my mind about is,' went on Markakis solemnly, 'what part *I* am intended to play by fate – for you can't deny it *was* fate that I should be there all the time. I am the only person, *I* suppose, who knows the whole story.' He seized Gilbert's arm, and his black eyes glittered. 'It should have been you, not me. But listen, and I'll tell you... That's why I say – you are never on the spot, you know. Is it accident or have you a sort of wilful blindness? It's so strange that in *my* country a man would be thought a half-wit who behaved as you do, whereas apparently here it's considered the height of civilization...'

Gilbert watched him unflinchingly. 'Go on,' he said. 'What was the story you were going to tell me?'

Markakis settled himself more comfortably, leaning against the closed piano. 'It's the story of the dagger,' he began portentously. 'It's the dagger you must think of as the hero. Never mind the people. Listen.' He swung round quickly, opened the piano, and in crashing chords, played the sword-theme from *The Ring*. 'The sword – no, the dagger. We could alter the phrase a little, to make it stand for the dagger. Listen again.' He played it again with some slight changes. 'Let that stand for the dagger. I saw her give it to him.'

He was about to play this likewise, but Gilbert swung him round. 'Who gave it to whom?' he said sharply. 'Damn your playing and your posing. Tell the thing straightforwardly, if you aren't too drunk, you –'

Markakis stared at him, gently reproachful. His dark lock of hair hung in a crescent on his forehead, as if he were a victim stamped with the sign of some oriental goddess. 'You should let me tell you in music,' he said; 'I could say it better that way. I *will*.' Gilbert held him by the arms; he struggled violently for a minute, but he could not manage to turn back to the piano. 'Never mind,' he said to himself softly, 'I shall play it, some day. So that all the world shall be *glad* to hear. Many others will play it, and marvel – wonder where I got that theme. I can keep it in my head until I can get manuscript paper. First there is the dagger itself,' He paused, as if listening to the phrase. 'Did you hear it?' He laughed. 'No, of course not, you are deaf as well as blind. If I played it fifty times you would never hear it. It is the soul that hears, and "What good are eyes and ears, if the soul be barbarous?" Then' – he listened again. Gilbert waited, still gripping him by the forearms. 'Then,' went on Markakis, his face suddenly suffused with happiness, 'there is the princess. That's easy. I got her long ago, when first she entered this room. The princess gives the dagger to Marcus.

I must be very careful not to sentimentalize that. How do I know why she gave it to him? It looked like a love-gift. I hope it was. He is a man. He was wasted on Claribel. But still, I don't know that she gave it him out of love. That is what one would naturally assume in this sentiment-ridden country. She might have given it to him as what it is – a weapon, to plunge into the heart of an enemy. At any rate, he went straight to Claribel, didn't he? The light went on in the studio.'

Where were *you*? said Gilbert. 'Eavesdropping again?'

'I?' said Markakis surprised. 'Didn't I tell you? I was below, in the garden. I saw Marcus and the princess just before they went in. And then the light went on in the studio. I heard them talking and arguing – him and Claribel. I didn't hear what they said. I didn't wish to. I was brooding on what I had just seen. In fact, I didn't come to life until they came out on the balcony, and the dagger came flying through the air and fell beside the path out there. Poor Marcus! He hadn't reckoned on the cunning of the woman.'

His face changed, and his eyes grew fixed, as if he were still staring at the shining dagger lying on the ground.

'Go on,' said Gilbert, shaking him. 'What did they do then?'

'Never mind them,' said Markakis impatiently. 'Think of the dagger. There it is, on the path, you see. The light from the studio was shining on it. It was a perfect scene for an opera – the rhododendrons, and behind them the dark wood, and the yellow light – not all of it, the balcony cut off some – the slanting rays falling on the silver dagger. I couldn't slip out of the shadows' – he shook himself free of Gilbert's grip, and flung his arms up wildly. 'I was rooted to the spot, fascinated. Now I see why. I felt like the stage-manager, standing in the wing... The dagger lay there.'

Gilbert no longer tried to control him. He had escaped into an enchanted land where it was useless to try to follow him. Gilbert listened, trying to make sense, to gather the story from what were to him his irrelevant ravings.

'The dagger lay there, in a blaze of light. I stood and watched it, unable to make up my mind to go and take it. Think of the power that would have given me! How I could have played on their loves and hatreds, Marcus's and Claribel's! I could have promised it first to one and then to the other, and finally, I could have cheated them, and formally given it back to the Princess Lucy, who would then have remembered me, perhaps given me a letter, a command to play to her in her own country... But I didn't move. I see now, I could not, any more than the stage-manager can step forth on to the stage when the curtain has gone up. Everything was quiet. I waited. And then, just as one would expect, I heard voices, coming from the wood...'

He stretched out his left hand dramatically, in the manner of a conductor waiting to give the beat for the orchestra to begin.

'They came in,' he said, 'hand in hand – or have I invented that? I see it all so clearly – but is it what happened that I see, or my opera, fully formed? Ah well, whichever it is, it is best. I care nothing for reality. They came in. They at least were lovers. Oh, they *must* be. I must have that. I couldn't bear it otherwise. They are young and beautiful. You see, I can appreciate that, for I am young, but not beautiful.'

'Who came in?' said Gilbert. 'Who?'

'Theresa, the beautiful one, and her poet, of course,' answered Markakis mildly. 'Who else should it be? I wonder,' he broke off thoughtfully, 'if Sylens is *really* a poet? Do you think he is?' he said solemnly to Gilbert. 'He is a little too – English, too nice and gentlemanly, to be quite right for Theresa, who is a wild cat under all that marble beauty. *I* could have done better than he – but she would not look at me. I *have* beauty, but it is like that of

Socrates – it is all inside me, and the Graces have not granted me that my exterior should correspond with my inward parts. Well, no matter. In our opera we will *make* him a poet. Eh?'

He slipped away from the piano. Gilbert, fascinated, turned on the spot where he stood, to watch his antics.

'You see them then, the two lovers – the poet and the princess (I am *sure* she is a real princess, much more sure than that he is a real poet) approaching slowly from out of the dark wood. Hand in hand. You pass that?' Gilbert, hypnotized, nodded. 'The dagger lies on the dark ground It is bathed in light. They see it. She sees it first. Ah, what music, as she sees it! My dagger-theme, played on the flute and then on the wood-wind, with the violins rustling in the background, like Mendelssohn's in the overture to *A Midsummer Night's Dream*. She picks it up. She shows it to him. She tells him to whom it belongs. She in turn gives it to *her* lover to take care of for her. He swears to keep it – he swears it on his life. Just as the other had done, a little while before. They enter the dark house...'

He sighed and came back to Gilbert.

'So far, so good. The rest is interesting, but it's in a different mood. It is as if out of a different opera, a comedy of intrigue – Mozart perhaps. We cannot unite them. Let us make a second, then. I am seated here.' He was back at his place, leaning against the keyboard. Gilbert had not stepped out of his charmed circle, he revolved on his base, completely hypnotized by Markakis.

'I am seated here. I play. Opposite me is Marcus Praed. I play, and I know what he is thinking: he is wondering where is the dagger. For he has been down to look for it, you see, and so has Claribel. I saw them. Oh, it was funny!' Markakis' shoulders shook with laughter. 'One after the other, they came and searched. Imagine their surprise!... However, here I sit and play, knowing what he is thinking. Presently Claribel comes to him, and they talk. They are sure I don't hear – I am absorbed in my playing as usual – and if I do, I shan't understand. But I do, they couldn't be so allusive that I wouldn't follow them, every innuendo. It was like being a child again, and hearing my grandfather spell the words he didn't wish me to hear – whereas of course, I understood the spelling too. He threatened her. She defied him. But I think she's beaten really – she will try to get it for him if she can.'

'Do they know who has it?' said Gilbert.

'No, no. They don't know. Only I know and, of course, the Princess Theresa. That's why Marcus wants to play another game of murder-party. He will get it back then, if he has to tear the clothes off all of them. Claribel will help, probably. But meanwhile, Sylens is guarding it for his princess. So you see what a scramble this next game is going to be – unless, of course, Sylens plays the little gentleman and returns it.'

'Is that all?' said Gilbert.

Markakis, sunk into a reverie or a stupor, seemed to have forgotten his presence. He stood with his chin on his chest, scowling at the ground. Gilbert too stood still for a few moments longer, and then turned away and began piling plates again.

Neither of them noticed Betty, who had been for some while standing in the doorway, and now slipped quietly away.

## 29

Claribel had not been looking for Lucy's dagger. She had been lying on her bed.

There was nothing unusual in this for her. Often, even at her own parties, the desire to be alone came over her, and no foolish sense of duty towards her guests restrained her from following it. She was, by impulse, sociable; always she collected her personnel with the utmost care and enthusiasm; and she looked forward to the resultant evening with an ever-renewed, childlike eagerness. She hoped for pleasure, that special pleasure without which she could not live: and for a while she obtained it. The company assembled here to-night: what had they in common, at the outset, except their interest in her? It was really necessary to her that every single person in the room should have his or her attention fixed upon Claribel. Then, warmed and illuminated by these centripetal rays, she was at her best; she could shine back upon them all effortlessly and impartially. But the moment any one of her entourage turned his mind elsewhere, Claribel was immediately aware of a lack, as if a light had failed and the room had gone a little darker. Then, to the surprise of her friends, who were perhaps enjoying themselves and saw nothing wrong, Claribel would feel tired, and complain that the party was not going well, she couldn't think why, and so the party would find itself voluntarily breaking up, though no one knew when or how the chill had descended. Sometimes Claribel found it sufficient to retire for a while, until she was missed and sought for. By this method many gatherings at her house had been brought to their senses...

But to-night it was different.

For the first time in her experience, Claribel was aware that the situation was out of her control. No breaking-up of the party, no retirement would avail here; as for the former, she doubted whether it could be done. Who would accept her suggestion that it wasn't worth continuing? It was probable that whatever she said, whatever she did, would pass completely unheeded. She had, for instance, been here now for half an hour or more, and no one, not even Gilbert, had come to seek her out. Possibly they had not even noticed her absence.

No, she had retired, not to create her usual sensation – a depression, a sense of loss, in the company – but to think. It was Claribel's principle never to have recourse to thought unless this could not be avoided; she had a low opinion of the intellect, and of intellectual methods: she had always relied on opportunism for the solution of her problems, and she had so far had no reason to be dissatisfied with her choice. She was never tired of ridiculing people who tried to live by reason; and undermining their carefully built-up theories was one of her favourite pastimes. But she was logical, all the same: her opportunism was consistent, and she recognized full well that there came a time when the intellect had to be called in, when nothing less than a careful survey of the situation would save it. It was distasteful and tiresome, and she shirked it till the last possible moment. She could certainly count the number of times in her life when she had been driven to the length of 'thinking things out'. But she always knew when such a crisis had arrived; she knew it now.

What had happened?

Before she began this momentous process of thinking, she had to prepare herself, to work up to it by slow steps; and meanwhile to keep her mind a blank, to forget everything, even the immediate task, and pretend that nothing unusual lay ahead of her. And so first she took a hot bath – for it was one of Gilbert's duties to see that the boiler in the basement was well stoked, so that the supply of hot water never failed – and in it she put twice the usual amount of bath salts. These were of the kind that not only scent, but colour the water; and so Claribel lay for ten minutes in turquoise-green water that gave off a fragrance like that of the most scented of white lilies. Then she powdered her body, which was still smooth and firm and unwrinkled as a girl's; and reset her blonde hair in its crisp, glistening waves. For the rest of her toilet, she moved to her ever-heated bedroom; but she did not spend as much time as usual over the restoration of her maquillage, for she was driven onward by her secret purpose, the desire to *think*.

At last, having dressed herself in a white silk Russian shirt with a high collar, and black silk trousers, she climbed on to the bed. But even now she had to take care – to 'hasten slowly.' And so, switching on the light above her bed's head, she picked up a novel from the side table, and lay at full length, pretending to herself that she was going to read. Perhaps she still hoped to escape the necessity of thinking – to get absorbed in the book, or to be interrupted, or to go to sleep... However, it was useless. Her eyes followed the lines for half a page, but no sense penetrated to her mind. The worst had come to the worst. She laid down the novel with a sigh, and lying on her back, and staring up at the ceiling, she began...

## 30

'My party, so carefully arranged, designed to give me even more satisfaction than any of its predecessors: why has it got out of hand? What is wrong?'

Claribel's forehead was not wrinkled, even when she thought. No one would have guessed, to see her lying there, apparently full of repose, that she was thinking. Perhaps some people would not have given this title to Claribel's mental activity; but it was what she meant by the word, and our definitions don't always agree. Claribel's problem was as important to her as the problem of Pure Being was to Kant and Aristotle, and she gave it her fullest attention. Nothing could divert her, now that she had embarked; if anyone came to seek her out, she would be lost in contemplation, alone with her Ego, as some human beings like to feel themselves alone with their God.

What had gone Wrong? Was it in the original selection? She went over her party one by one, taking the better-known quantities first.

Gilbert: of course his presence was inevitable, and she would not ordinarily have wasted time over him; but to-night, everything must be taken into consideration, for everything seemed to be behaving slightly out of character. Even Gilbert had had his little surprises. For instance, why was he not anxious over her disappearance? As a rule she could not absent herself for five minutes without his coming to see if anything was wrong. And then there

was his display of spitefulness just now, here in this room. She was
used to his occasional fits of jealous despair. Naturally, because
he loved her, he thought everyone else was bound to do the same;
equally naturally, he was bound to wish sometimes either that they
did not, or that it should not matter to her. In these moods, though
violent, he was always manageable, because his own conscience,
his code, worked against him, and she was quick to seize this
advantage. Of course, she could not have told him the *whole* truth
about the many men who had not been able to help falling in love
with her; that would have been selfish, would have given Gilbert
unnecessary pain. Even now, after all these years, he was not quite
accustomed to the thought even of Marcus; sometimes his practised
resignation, his chivalrous code, would break down, and he would
take her – it was rather pathetic, really – into his confidence as if
she were a third party. He had no one else to tell, he reminded her;
and he spoke because silence would be dangerous – for her. Poor
Gilbert! Always his thought was of her. His violence was never
directed at her, nor even at Marcus, whom he liked and admired: it
was a beating of the hands against the bars of self. Claribel did not
quite understand, but she appreciated the value of such characters
in this wicked world; not for anything would she have allowed his
self-sacrifice to be wasted by any foolish refusal to avail herself
of it. The only thing was, Gilbert did not know, and she did not
mean to tell him, the full extent of his generosity...

It was true that she would rather he didn't find this out; but
this was because the discovery would give him fresh pain, and
might even prove too much for him, so that he was forced to spoil
his ideal picture of himself as thinking only of her happiness. She
didn't want Gilbert to blot his copybook. But fear lest he should
find out weighed very little with her; she believed in her power to
manage him, even if he found out the whole. Take this evening:

he had undoubtedly caught her kissing Desmond, and he had undoubtedly been annoyed. But had she felt afraid? Not a bit. And she had been justified: when she had explained, he had collapsed at once and apologized. She could always think of a way of putting things, even the truth, so that Gilbert would be disarmed, would be made to feel that he was being selfish.

No: she could never fear Gilbert's jealousy. If ever he made himself unbearable, she had always the simple resource of leaving him. She believed that this threat would still, and for ever, be sufficient to bring him to heel; but if it were not, she could act on it. In some ways it would be a relief: Gilbert, angelic as he was, bored her a little, of course. She definitely shunned being left alone with him; but then, she always had, except in the very beginning when she had thought he had to be won. He had looked difficult; people said he was, and that had attracted her. But at the first touch – he didn't fall, he *leapt*... As she idly turned over in her mind these early days with Gilbert – oh, how dim and distant they seemed! – she was aware that she was coming to the point, or rather circling round it; for somewhere embedded in these meditations there was an unpleasantness, something small but real, and quite new, otherwise she would not have been thinking about him at all. She shrank from it, yet she sought it, and the knowledge of its existence affected her like the discovery of the first crow's foot or the first grey hair. It was trifling in itself; but it was a one-way change, and the harbinger of more.

What was it, then? It brought fear, though not for the reason she had given Marcus. She had told Marcus that Gilbert might kill her if she stayed; but that had been melodramatics, partly due to a desire to move Marcus, and partly arising out of her own confusion of mind. For one thing, she did not greatly fear death; everyone knew that about Claribel. She combined with sensuousness a remarkable absence of physical fear, which her admirers called courage and her detractors called a lack of imagination. She could swim miles out to sea, do stunts in an aeroplane, face a madman waving a revolver, with extraordinary calm, not the calm of self-control but of indifference. This in itself would be sufficient to prevent Gilbert, even if jealousy did drive him insane, from ever laying a finger on her. She knew it. And yet when she had said that to Marcus, though the form in which she had expressed her fear was untrue, yet there had been fear to express. Fear of what, then? She struggled to find the answer, and for the first time a tiny fold appeared on her brow.

Slowly, reluctantly, she let the portrait of Gilbert – his mask – form itself on the dark background of her closed eyes, and his voice, that thin spiteful voice with the new note in it, creep again into her ears, as she had heard it an hour or two ago in this same room. 'Twelve years is a long time… Marcus is a dark horse. You've long since given up watching him *your natural vanity makes you blind*… The onlooker sees most of the game.'

That was it. That was it. The realization was upon her, like the spring of a feline that fells one to the ground. It was not his telling her that Marcus would fail her: that might have been love, the desire to protect her as of old. It was that underneath his statement there was triumph: suppressed glee, that rubbed its hands over the well-earned fate that was coming to her. That one sentence: 'Your natural vanity makes you blind'; even at the moment it had struck her as incongruous, as if someone else, not Gilbert, were speaking. Never in all their life together, whatever the provocation, whatever his pain, had he uttered the slightest word of criticism against her, before that phrase.

So it had happened. The one-way change had taken place: love into, not hatred, but dislike, pure, cold, critical dislike, against which she knew she would be powerless. Gilbert was lost. Yet even that was not the worst; she could do without Gilbert, though she felt very differently about it now that there was a possibility of his abandoning her, now that the choice was not solely in her hands. She could do without him, though she would miss his silent service, in great things and small, and his presence which shielded her from the world's cruder criticisms. The thing that chilled her with this new kind of fear was the realization that if she had lost him, there was nothing she was not capable of losing, and that might soon have to be amended to, nothing she was capable of keeping.

Her luck, her marvellous luck that had allowed her to ignore all rules and still succeed, had broken at last. And that brought her to the content of what Gilbert had said; for not only had he wished it to be true, he had been proved right, startlingly soon. The eyes of ill will had been no less sharp than the eyes of loving kindness. '*I* watch him always…' With a sudden thrill not unlike pleasure, Claribel wondered: did Gilbert hate Marcus too? Had he, actually, never done other than hate them both? And was that the really basic cause of her fear, that all through these years she had mistaken hate for love? 'Your natural vanity makes you blind.'

But her thoughts, following a deeply secret plan that was not of her devising, were beginning to leave Gilbert and turn to Marcus.

M arcus.

Claribel's marvellous visual memory, her one true gift, set him before her, in every attitude, at every age down through the years she had known him. She saw him first as she had fallen in love with him, one day when she and Gilbert were meeting him outside a concert hall. It was a bitterly cold winter's afternoon, with sleet falling. Marcus had just driven up in an open car and he wore no overcoat. She admired him, as one admires a lion, for his physical development, which gave him a certain beauty of stance, of skeletal and muscular arrangement; she had often tried, and sometimes succeeded, in expressing that arrangement in stone. He had no facial beauty; his face, even at that age, was definitely plain, though his head was well set on his shoulders. But what most attracted her, what gave her a real thrill as she stepped, muffled in sables, out of her own closed car, was the knowledge that this man combined great physical strength with subtlety of character. She knew that he would lead her a dance before, and perhaps even after, she ensnared him...

And so he had.

How had he managed, without any of the usual tricks, to hold her interest over all these years, when so many others had failed? He had made no secret of his intentions; he had never pretended to less than he felt, nor had he tried to hold her by trying to make her feel unsure of him. He had let her know, quite early, that he regarded himself as pledged to her, and that that promise would stand, unless – unless what? He had certainly wanted a great deal in return; he was no cavalier servant, like poor Gilbert. He expected her, if she loved him, to show it without fear or chicanery. He respected her misgivings about Gilbert, but only because he believed her to be genuinely fond of Gilbert; he would have had no patience with mere prudence, which he would not have understood, for he himself had none; and if she had pleaded duty, he would not have believed her. And so he took her, with the full knowledge and actually the consent of Gilbert. She doubted whether he realized that he ought to consider Gilbert, much less be grateful to him for a sacrifice. He himself expected to get from life only what he had fairly won and could keep; it would never have occurred to him to give way of his own accord, in any situation. But if he were defeated, he would accept it with amazing calm, because it would be simply defeat, no more, and he would not be bearing anyone a grudge for an incapacity purely his own. Voluntary acts of sacrifice are sprats to catch mackerel, so he thought. In a sense, he had no conscience; and so, if subtle intellectually, ethically he was simple. Claribel liked that. She found it exhilarating not to have to consider Marcus, to know that he was well able to look after himself.

Why did he like her?

Claribel had a high opinion of her ability to charm, and for this she had excellent support: an unbroken line of successes. She had succeeded with Marcus, as with the rest; she had meant to, and expected to. And yet, when it happened, she was surprised. She could not quite believe it, in the completeness of it; and she never had. There appeared to be no reason why she should doubt, when she saw her lion roll in a silken net at her feet; but – what was it? – did the lion's eye roll a little too dramatically? Wasn't he a little too helpless, too overcome, for such a big lion in such a frail net? In short, was his tongue in his cheek as he gazed up at his dear mistress? Claribel's sense of humour was far from strong; she seldom saw herself as even potentially ridiculous, but there had been times when she had wondered whether Marcus was pulling her leg, playing a long, complex, secret game in which she had a part that would stagger her if she knew it. The game was very serious, for him, it had rules. But he alone knew them, and he played alone. Was it possible, for instance, that Marcus had a scheme of living, and that in this scheme there had to be among other things one great love affair, just as some people's scheme of interior decoration demands a large vase with one flower in it, against such and such a wall?

Still, even if this were the whole truth, it was none the less a compliment that he had chosen her for the part; it was, in fact, a superb compliment, that of one artist to another, and not to be compared with the facile victories of sexual attraction, which are largely the result of propinquity. The course of the ordinary love affair is terribly swift and painfully predictable. Marcus had always been full of surprises. And yet – she kept returning to this, his most wonderful quality in her eyes – though he was subtle, he was also robust. He gave, and took, all that other men did; he was no unsatisfactory worshipper at a distance, too much engrossed in his own idea of the beloved object to see that she was a human being like himself, with desires and purposes and wishes as strong as his own. Claribel knew all about those. Carraway and Sylens, for instance, both charming, both artists, had a dash of that futility about them. She had enjoyed her love affairs with each of them, but only because she had Marcus, a real man, as well. Otherwise they would have exasperated her, with their passion for arranging life instead of experiencing it... Marcus had schemes and theories, but unlike the poet and the painter he kept them to himself. He did not force them on the attention of the object. He played his private game quite secretly, and left her to be herself. The result was that though she could have written a book on the *Weltanschauung* of either Sylens or Carraway, she had no more idea of Marcus' innermost beliefs than on the day she first met him.

Yes, it was like that that she still saw him: as a torso, half-turned away, strong without brutality, simple without naïveté, subtle without futility. She had done portraits, in one medium or another, of all her men: of Gilbert, her greatest success was a certain mask in bronze of which he himself had once said in a lighter moment that it was like a sick cat; but Marcus was the only one who had required a life-size study in stone. She had done him naked, in green stone, because when she had seen him that first day, he had happened to be wearing a suit of green tweed, which, as his clothes were usually rather ill-kept – or was it because no clothes could for long flatten out his irrepressible lines? – had seemed to mould itself to his form. That statue had made her internationally famous, at least among sculptors. It stood in a certain London art gallery, and it amused her sometimes to go and watch other people looking at it... 'Mine,' she would think, smiling, 'for ever and ever, *mine.*'

At this, a stab of pain went through her, the sharpest she had ever known. Again, she was faced with the intensely disagreeable in her thoughts; and this time she had come upon it so suddenly that there was no chance to evade it, to brace oneself, to pretend it wasn't there until one was fully prepared. She had lost Marcus. The event itself had been sudden, a stepping off solid ground into an abyss. At the beginning of the evening, he had still been hers. She had lost Marcus. How? How? The three sisters? They would have been powerless if something she herself had done hadn't sold them the pass. What could that have been?

She rolled over on the bed, trying to remember. There was nothing – nothing that had not been true for years and years – for so long that she had given up considering it as at all extraordinary or in any way the concern of Marcus. If he found out, she could always say to him, 'You found no difference in me, did you? Was I any the less charming? Did you therefore really lose anything? Then why should you care?' That was flawless reasoning. Marcus was and always had been incurious. It was therefore his fault if he knew less than he wished to know. She could not be expected to tell him things he did not ask. She asked *him* no questions...

But to-night, it seemed, she was not to be allowed the luxury of deceiving herself. An inexorable voice in herself kept pulling her back, the moment she pretended to know less than the truth. For the truth was that she was not, and never had been, the woman for Marcus. He had chosen her, and she had served his purpose well enough; he would not, she felt sure, blame her for any short-comings, or rather any failure to correspond exactly with his idea. But he had always known, quite calmly and clearly, that she was a makeshift, a second best. And to-night, for some reason, he had decided to act on the knowledge.

Probably she would never discover that reason, what it was. But what devilment of fate was it that had caused her to bring to the house, and set before him, the woman who had by a natural right stepped into her place? For the Princess Lucy was that woman: she saw it now with painful clearness. What irony in the thought that all these years she had been merely keeping the Princess Lucy's bed warm!

But she did not wish, yet, to think of the three princesses. Her mind with a jerk leapt away from Marcus. There was a minute or two of blackness; and the next thing she saw forming itself on the dark curtain was the grinning mask of Markakis.

## 32

Markakis. As his face leered at her, near her own, she found herself sitting upright on the bed, gazing back at it with hatred and fury. She would have spat into it had she been really deluded; but she was not insane, and she knew the difference between percept and fantasy. But there he was, his dark eyes with that veiled, drugged look, his lock of hair falling on the forehead, his smile. How could she ever have thought to make a friend of him, the little Cretan boy! He was as untamable as a panther, and as treacherous. She had thought to make him eat out of her hand; and he had done so, watching her all the while, looking for a nice soft spot on her white flesh in which to sink his teeth... Where had her wits been wandering, not to see that for every time she had humiliated him, every gramophone record she had made him play, every use she had put him to, helping Gilbert, providing her guests with music as a background for their conversation, he had made a notch in his mind until the day of reckoning had come. She believed that if the fancy took him he would kill her. She was glad that that dagger had not fallen into *his* hands, while she was beside him...

What had made her collect him? She had never liked him. But she had recognized his genius, and what was more, recognized it inwardly, with her usual perception. She had made a leering mask of him, in dark wood, that was really bacchanal, frightening in its intensity. She had robbed him of his boy friend, who flattered him; she had made him choose between them. And then she had suddenly got tired of the game. Why? Because she had recognized that Markakis, alone, friendless, a foreigner for all his English education, Markakis stripped of everything except his genius, was nevertheless self-sufficient, indomitable, beyond the power of such as she. The utmost she had ever done to him was to scratch the surface. True, he had wept before her uncontrollably, poured out his most intimate thoughts, thrown dignity to the winds, followed her like a dog with a dog-like look in his eyes, obeyed her most unreasonable demands, abased himself with an abandon that she had found indecent; and all for nothing, for of course she could not give him what he wanted. She preferred him where he was... And yet, in spite of it all, her power over him was nil. He was a southerner; that was how he reacted to any woman who happened to set a match to his highly inflammable nature; and furthermore, almost any attractive woman was liable to do that. He was not a philanderer; he was not playing at love, for he did not know the meaning of love, in the western sense. He knew the disturbance of an animal in spring, and the abandon of his behaviour meant no depth of passion; it expressed merely the urgency of a need that if satisfied would pursue a swift and normal course through pleasure to, not exactly indifference, but forgetfulness. Her crime had been that of the owner of a domestic pet who keeps it indoors...

Yet was even that the whole truth? No. Markakis did know the meaning of love; he was capable of devotion, and even of ordinary friendliness. He had loved his friend, though a temporary disturbance had driven friendship out of the lists; he admired Marcus, and could, she believed, have loved him if Marcus had ever paid him any attention. He even liked Gilbert; they got on well together in a queer silent way, and Markakis' acts of service were not altogether unwilling when they involved helping Gilbert. In short, was there anyone he didn't like, except herself? She had watched him this very evening, talking to the Princess Lucy; he had seemed quite happy then. No... it was herself he hated, and all the antics she put him through could never make him do other than despise her. She had made a mistake there; she should have avoided at all costs the easy appeal, and treated him, of all people, sexlessly, as an artist. If Sylens was a little less than a man, and must therefore be treated as one and not as the poet and scholar in which he loved to take refuge, then Markakis, by the same reasoning, should have been approached by way of his mind.

Another lost opportunity! But he must go now; he must be got rid of quickly, before he was given the chance to do her any harm. She would start again; she would have new friends. All these were tainted. At her next New Year's Eve party, not one of them would appear, except Dione and poor George, who had somehow wandered out of another world into this one, and were interested in each other only. And even they must go, because though harmless in themselves, they would for ever remind her of this horrible evening. And that tiresome Irishman, who came here to get a cheap meal and pick up a cheap girl; and clumsy, vacuous Desmond, and shrewd vulgar Peggy and suburban Betty; all, all must go. Carraway and Sylens: she had been tired of both of them for a long time now, but at the thought of their desertion this evening her hands clenched and she drew a sharp breath –

And so, again without warning, her mind leapt away, and behold, she was staring into the smiling, slightly disdainful, finely modelled faces of Ursula, Lucy, and Theresa.

## 33

The three sisters.

By what madness of bravado had she invited them here to-night? Oh, they had caught her, neatly enough... They knew her little weaknesses. They had made a study of them, no doubt. It was she who had asked them; it was they who had limed the twig on which she had finally alighted to pipe her expected song. Yes, when she had seen in the paper that they were in London, she had half thought of approaching them; and then she had remembered that this year in London was not the same thing as six years ago in Paris, and she had not dared. Had not dared! 'My God, my God,' thought Claribel, 'why didn't those words suggest the link to me? What had happened to my memory? What made me think that women of their race, their caste, would ever forget? But it seemed all different, in England, and now that they have got back their titles and their country – almost all they want, for people say it's only a matter of time before the monarchy is restored – why should they bother with small fry like me?'

Paris, six years ago, was full of distinguished refugees. Claribel had been working there, in two ways. Oh, what scope there was for an artist! The marvellous faces one saw! She had never known that Europe contained so many strange faces. Why bother about the other continents? One could never exhaust this one. She lived in an orgy of portraiture, thrilled like a lover by every new combination of features that expressed the innumerable families into which the human race has divided. She became expert at discerning ancestry; and though she never bothered to study, she could often surprise savants by her quick perception. She worked hard with her hands, and her skill and reputation grew. She became the fashion, and clients flocked to her studio. Gilbert was there, silently helping to make things run smoothly; Marcus was away on a dangerous excursion into the Antarctic. She had all she wanted, nothing she didn't want. But for an error of judgement she would be there now, busy, rich, famous. What had made her try her hand at that other game?

The three princesses, though in exile, were not poor. They had a house at Fontainebleau, where they entertained the cream of society. It was Claribel's art, not her connexions, that gained her an entrance. When she was asked to portray the sisters, she was thrilled, partly by the greatness of their name, partly by their nationality, which had for her a strong emotional appeal, and most of all because of themselves. She had an excellent idea of their appearance, for they were often photographed, and when she saw them, her impression was confirmed; they represented for her all that was romantic. She went quite wild about them; she gave herself up to the work, and everything, everybody else was neglected. Drawing was not her strong point; she preferred to model directly. But for the sake of the three sisters, she learnt to draw, to the best of her ability; she had decided, the moment she saw them, that the third dimension must be sacrificed to colour, that she must portray them in oils. She had never before risked her reputation on a commissioned work in oils; but she followed where her artistic conscience led. Day after day, the three sisters sat to her; she wooed them, severally and together. She made friends with the youngest, Theresa; and at first this seemed easy. Theresa at eleven had the same perfect beauty as now, and a grace of manner that led one to believe oneself as charming as she pretended; Claribel walked with her in the forest, rode with her, took her for drives… It was some time before she discovered that her sole function in Theresa's eyes was to provide an occasional escape from a life rigidly mapped out by Ursula. Claribel was preferable to the governess, the music mistress, and the dancing master, that was all. Claribel, offended, dropped the child…

Next she tried Ursula. But Ursula was too clever for her, and too fanatical. Her mind was embittered by her parents' death, and the political disaster that had overtaken her dynasty. Ursula was busy, always receiving visitors, considering dispatches, plotting, planning, waiting, and bringing up her sisters. She had no time for Claribel, and Claribel, repelled by her concentration of purpose, her indifference to what was merely personal, soon gave up the attempt to hold her own with Ursula. She nicknamed her 'The Prime Minister' among her own associates, and rather spitefully mimicked her for their amusement. But her portrait of Ursula had nothing of caricature; it was grave, dignified, and beautiful, for Claribel's hand was forced to obey the integrity of her vision, and the moment she looked at Ursula as a subject for her art, all attempt to belittle her was forgotten. Her personal feeling of dislike and irritation had to be kept outside.

Last, she tried Lucy. She had, with her usual lack of judgement, thought Lucy the least interesting of the three. Lucy had not Ursula's impressiveness nor Theresa's beauty. She was quiet, and seemed to take less interest than they did in the past glories of her race, or in the lure of the present. But as she studied her, the pale complexion, the dark hair, the fine nose, it began to dawn on her that Lucy had after all the greatest possibilities of the three. She was so much cleverer than she seemed, so much more observant, so much more reckless. Claribel tried to tempt her out of the safe circle guarded by Ursula; and for a time she succeeded. It had to be done very warily, because of Ursula's loving, suspicious eye; and because of Lucy's sense of duty; for, Claribel discovered, Lucy already saw herself as the most active of the three, destined in time to protect and save them, to do a great work in the world. Claribel, by a display of affection, got her alone, got her to talk...

What a pity she hadn't left it at that. But then, there had been Raymond.

## 34

'What did I do, after all?' thought Claribel. 'I didn't know. I merely brought her and Raymond together. I didn't know what a treacherous little beast he was.'

Yes, by devious ways, Claribel had arranged that Lucy should meet Raymond – to please Raymond, of course. He wanted a new sensation: a young girl, a princess, so grave and charming and unaware of the wickedness of the world. Had he been in love with her? Probably. He said he was; he convinced Claribel. Had Lucy fallen in love with Raymond? She would have been less than human if she hadn't; everybody did. And Claribel, who liked bringing people together, who cared not a straw for the divinity that hedges princesses, and who bore Ursula a mild grudge besides, went to infinite trouble to arrange a first meeting in her studio. The rest arranged itself: a few 'chance' meetings elsewhere, when she and Lucy were out dining together, and the damage was done. The next time Claribel found it imperative to her separate portrait of Lucy that the sitting should take place at her own studio, Claribel was not there. But Raymond was. He had suborned Lucy's duenna, of course. He was a very rich young man, and very charming...

A few days later when Claribel went to the house at Fontainebleau to keep her appointment, she was shocked to find it closed. She learnt that the princesses had left for an indefinite period, and no one knew their destination. Later she read that they were staying with relatives in some castle among the Carinthian hills. Raymond too had disappeared.

During the next month or so, Claribel found that many of her more distinguished clients had left Paris for unknown destinations. It was the time of year when people do leave Paris; still, it was odd that they should have omitted to let her know, especially as they usually left her with an unfinished portrait of some kind on her hands. She had another stratum of acquaintances; but when she tried to get news out of them, they all were vague....

At last Gilbert suggested that it was time they too went for a sea trip. He put it to her so diffidently, with such obvious tact that she could have murdered him; and if there had been any loophole, she would have refused. But she realized that if she didn't go now there was worse in store. So she went; and after the sea trip they felt an unspoken longing for London. There they settled, and Claribel's stock began to rise again. She found it possible to forgive the princesses for their unkindness, though a less reasonable person would have borne a grudge; what greater crime can one commit against an artist than to rob him of what might have been his greatest creation? Claribel kept her sketches and her canvases of the princesses, and from time to time she added a few touches. Her memory was perfect: their faces were stamped on her mind; every detail of their attitude, their hands, their very gestures – she could conjure them up at will. But when she tried to set this on canvas, she failed. The three seemed to sit together, proud Ursula, beautiful Theresa, and Lucy, whose gravity covered a wildness, almost ferocity, that was quite clear to Claribel now, and should have been clear always. They sat together – no breaking that circle, really – as if in judgement on her. She could see Ursula bend down to speak to Lucy, not harshly, but with a grave trust and tenderness, and Lucy's quick smile that faded as suddenly as it came. Theresa, unaware, leaned back against her sister's knee, in confident calm. What did Ursula say to Lucy, and what did Lucy reply? Claribel saw them thus in dreams, by day and by night, and she wondered. Had Raymond seduced Lucy? Who had given them away? Had they been watched? Was it possible that Raymond, in thinking he could bribe their servants, had been making the mistake of his life?

Claribel persisted in thinking that she had done no harm. That was why she could not bring herself to finish the portrait of the three of them: how could she face what grew up under her hands – her three judges? Yet it would have had a remarkable value. No one rejoiced more than she did when the news of their restoration startled Europe. They were being held now, under a kind of regency, until one of them should marry, it appeared. It didn't matter which, so long as the line was continued; and people believed that the two other sisters would give way to whichever of them married first. Rumour fastened on each of them in turn. Claribel's pleasure in their good fortune was untainted, however, by any mercenary motive; she wished them well, she had a sentimental regard for them, and as far as she was concerned, the past was forgotten.

Shortly afterwards she heard news of Raymond. He had foolishly wandered over the borders of their country and had been shot as a spy. At his flat in Paris much incriminating literature was discovered. Claribel was aghast. How could she have guessed that Raymond was in the anti-dynastic camp, actually in the pay of the three sisters' enemies? She saw it all now: the plot to get hold of Lucy, either to seduce her and get her to talk, or perhaps kidnap her or worse. So that was it! Imagine such a charming young man, whose only faults had seemed to be those one could so easily pardon! Claribel shuddered to think how grossly she had been deceived, how basely she had been used. She was almost minded to write Lucy a letter of congratulation, in which she would explain her own innocence. But Gilbert persuaded her to refrain.

It had been doubly gratifying, therefore, when they had

approached her. She had been so graciously received that she had found herself, in a burst of gratitude and heroine-worship, putting into words what seemed impossible of fulfilment: her desire that they should grace her New Year's Eve party. They had looked at one another, just as she had so often seen them in her imaginings, and smilingly consented. Her spirits had soared. Not only would she be able to show them to her guests; she would perhaps be able at last to finish the famous picture, since they no longer seemed to be judging her. Perhaps they had never done so at all. Perhaps they had not known her part in the arrangement; or else, understanding her comparative innocence, had excused. The sudden approach of a danger, which Ursula with her inside knowledge of political intrigue would appreciate, must have been the cause of their departure without leaving word. They saw in her nothing but a talented artist, an acquaintance of those Parisian days when their fortunes were still under a cloud.

All was well. They would not have come otherwise. She was tired and nervy; the trying time she had had this evening with Gilbert and Marcus and Markakis had upset her, filled her with absurd alarms. In a few minutes she would rejoin the party, and finish it off well, as it had begun. The princesses would want to be leaving soon; they had told her of their arrangements, and she had been flattered to notice that their visit to herself would be their last engagement before leaving England. They had called on her, as it were, on their way to the aerodrome.

She lay back, contented with her reasoning, and closed her eyes, longing to see there the familiar image of the three sisters, which to-morrow, without the slightest doubt, she would convey finally on to the canvas. When she reopened her eyes she was startled to see the door handle turn and the door begin slowly to open.

But it was only Betty after all.

## 35

Claribel looked at Betty with distaste: she was disappointed. The thought of Betty bored her extremely; she had forgotten her existence, and that she had asked her to the party, and why. Yet Betty looked well, standing, tall and thin, in her black velvet frock, which merged with the black background of the corridor in such a way that her head and neck stood out as if dissevered, like the profiles on coins. Bored as she was, Claribel's eyes conveyed to her brain that the only way to portray Betty would be in low relief: marble, white porcelain or black, silver or bronze, the possible media flitted through her brain as she stared at the outline of Betty's high forehead and thin nose, and resented her intrusion. She had thought, when the door handle turned, it might be one of the people of whom she had been thinking; her thought had led her to a point where she would have given much to speak to, for instance, Lucy alone.

Betty, calm though she looked, was nevertheless confused: some impulse had led her here in search of Claribel, but she had forgotten why she had come. She was not embarrassed; she was not thinking of Claribel. The confusion was within; perhaps it was the wine, which had previously elated her to the point of action, and now was letting her down. Besides, she had stood for so long in that other doorway that her purpose had got lost, as it were, side-tracked by a new interest. She stayed rigid, half in and half out of the room, vaguely wondering what to do next; and might have recollected herself and closed the door quietly and gone away, if Claribel hadn't spoken sharply from the bed:

'Come in, come in; don't stand there letting in the draught. What do you want? Is anyone asking for me?'

That decided Betty. She obeyed, and came slowly forward, walking as if hypnotized. Claribel watched her in amazement. Betty came to a stop at the edge of the bed, and stood looking down at Claribel in a way Claribel didn't like. For one thing, it is undignified to lie flat on your back and stare up at the person who is almost immediately above you. Yet Claribel did not feel able to move. That pale mask fascinated her, somewhat unpleasantly: she thought of wax, which she hated. The girl looked like the Muse of tragedy. What was the matter with her? Why didn't she speak? Claribel longed to shatter her rigidity, to make her come to life; but something prevented her, as one fears to wake a sleep-walker.

'What do you want?' she said again, but with less assurance; her own voice sounded quite thin in her ears.

Then Betty's calm broke. Her mask crumpled up, as it were, into a thousand creases, her body bowed forward like a candle melting in summer heat, and she began to laugh, uncontrollably. Claribel found that horrible. As Betty drooped towards and over her, she held out the palms of her hands to push her away. But Betty recovered slightly, and swaying, fell into a sitting position beside Claribel on the bed. She was still laughing. When she got her breath she said:

'I've heard such a funny story. I must tell you. It's about a dagger.'

'A dagger!' Claribel shot upright. 'What do you mean? Whose dagger? Where did you see it? Is it found?'

Betty went on unheeding.

'They don't know *I'm* in the secret. I could tell the princess, or Marcus, or even Sylens.' She laughed again. 'That would make nearly everybody, wouldn't it, now that Markakis has told Gilbert? In fact, you know, Claribel, you seem to be about the only one of us who doesn't know.'

Claribel's head swam as she vainly tried to piece these names together. She tried to remember her cunning; but impatience to know, and fury with Betty, urged her on.

'Where *is* the dagger?' she said, gripping Betty's forearm. 'Tell me at once, you little viper, or I'll have you sent home, and you shall never come here again.'

'I don't care. I don't care,' sang Betty, rocking herself to and fro. Her voice was so loud that Claribel drew back apprehensively. 'I don't *want* to come here again. I hate you, Claribel. Everybody does really, once they get to know you. People say you are beautiful, but *I* don't think so. *I* think you have horrid sly eyes.' Betty was not looking at Claribel, so that she did not see Claribel's expression. Not that that would have deterred her; she was enjoying herself too much to care if the heavens fell.

'Thank you, Betty,' said Claribel mildly. 'I'm glad I know how you feel. *In vino veritas*. But surely your little bourgeois soul knows that it's not done to insult your hostess on the Dutch courage inspired by *her* champagne. However – carry on. Let's hear the rest. *Why* do you hate me? Which of my possessions is it you envy? Don't mind me: I like to see the human mind revealed in all its meanness. Go on, little girl. Which of my friends have you set your cap at, without results? Perhaps I could help you… Is it the gentle Carraway or the charming Sylens? Or has Markakis with his southern temperament got you down? I hope it isn't the dark, mysterious Gilbert, for I'm afraid even I could do nothing for you there: you see, he wouldn't look at anyone but myself, even if I asked him to...' She paused, to see the effects of her words: Betty was looking down at her long thin hands which were spread out on her knees; and Claribel thought that something of what she was saying had gone home. Was that not a flush slowly rising on Betty's fair neck and cheek? Yes, for now it was fading, leaving her paler than before. Claribel had a sudden inspiration. 'Don't tell me,' she said, 'that it's Marcus.'

Betty's lips parted, but no denial came. Claribel leaned forward, and taking the pointed chin in her hands, turned Betty's face towards her. Sharply as Betty repulsed her, Claribel had time to catch a glimpse of the storm raging within. She lay back on her pillows, laughing softly.

'My poor girl,' she said. 'My poor child.' She really did feel quite tenderly towards Betty for the moment. There was something piquant in the thought of this young girl, outwardly so prim and decorous, inwardly aflame with longing for the virile sophisticated Marcus. If he knew! Claribel had a mind to tell him. He might, probably would be, merely bored; but he might take it into his head to profit, and that would be a break for Betty, while it lasted. How was it that these apparently virginal girls were so robust in their selection? Claribel's memory was always bad; and for the moment she had forgotten what Marcus had said about the Princess Lucy. Perhaps she had not taken it seriously, or perhaps she relied upon her own charms and Lucy's impending absence to bring Marcus to his senses. She leaned forward again, and laid a hand on Betty's knee.

'Listen, Betty,' she said. 'You think you hate me; if you were a psychologist you'd know that that simply didn't count, under the circumstances. But in any case, *I* don't hate *you*. I should like to help you – I know how you feel.'

Betty was listening stonily; but Claribel felt she was gaining ground.

'I asked you here this evening,' she said, 'hoping you might meet someone you liked – someone of your own age, like Desmond or she failed to think of another name, so she hurried on: 'However, you like Marcus, and you are right. He's splendid. Now listen; if you will help me, I'll help you. I see you know all about the dagger. Who told you, by the way?'

Betty said nervously, 'No one did. I listened. Markakis was telling Gilbert. He was there all the time.'

'*Where?*' said Claribel sharply, almost forgetting her rôle.

'In the garden,' said Betty. 'He saw Lucy give it to Marcus, and he heard you and Marcus quarrelling, and then he saw the dagger come flying out.'

'Then it was he!' exclaimed Claribel. 'He has had it all the time! Oh, the sly little beast, and he was listening in just now at the piano when Marcus and I were talking. I'll *make* him give it up. I'll –'

'*He* hasn't got it,' interrupted Betty gloomily. '*He* didn't pick it up.'

'Well, who did?' cried Claribel, exasperated. Betty flickered a glance at her; it was clear that she was by no means off her guard. Claribel went on hurriedly: 'You see, dear, it would be very unpleasant for me if the princess lost anything so valuable in my home.' She paused; the ambiguity of that sentence struck her, and she admired herself for her quickness of perception. 'I gather you know who they are.' She paused again, impressed anew with the augustness of her guests. She *must* contrive to see Lucy alone, and make it all right before they left. Besides, she was curious to know if... 'If you will tell me, I shall do my best to help you and Marcus to become friends.'

Betty laughed heartily. 'You couldn't,' she cried, rudely. 'You don't count with him any more.'

This time Claribel gave up all attempt at finesse. She knew that it was useless. She gripped Betty's thin wrist, and her fingers and thumb met round it, so that the long crimson nails overwrapped.

'You beastly, sneaking, eavesdropping little wretch,' she hissed. 'Just what do you mean by that, now? I suppose you have been spying again – watching Marcus and the Princess Lucy, and drawing your own vulgar little conclusions. In your circle we all know a man can't look at another woman without being in love with her, and of course he can't possibly be interested in two women at the same time. Oh, I know your fantastic code, handed down generation after generation, and quite impervious to change or reason or even common sense...' She drew her breath sharply; she must not get embarked on this topic, or she would rave on indefinitely and never come to the point, 'You think because he likes Lucy I have no more power over him. Well, you'll see. I shall prevent *you* from ever seeing him again. He will do that much at my request, believe me.'

Betty sneered. 'Ah, but you don't know what *I* know.'

'What?' screamed Claribel, beside herself. 'If you don't give up hinting, I'll call Marcus himself and then we'll see how you'll face *him* with your stories.'

Betty got off the bed. 'What you don't know,' she said, calmly, 'is, *why* Marcus is through with you at last. He has done a little listening to other people's conversations too: he can't deny that. And I think he was interested, judging by results. Apparently he holds the same vulgar bourgeois views as I do. Funny that he happened to be sitting beside his princess when he heard what he wanted.'

She began to walk away towards the door. Claribel was beyond asking any further questions. If she had moved a finger, it would have been to hurl the first heavy object she could lay her hands on at Betty's head. At the door Betty turned.

'They were sitting behind us,' she said, 'at the beginning of the evening, when Peggy was putting me wise about your collection here. She happened to mention that all the men present were, or had been, or were marked down to be, your lovers. Marcus heard... It seems it was news to him. The princess heard too, of course. Since then, as you see, they're inseparable. I should think there was some connexion, shouldn't you? Anyhow, if you're not afraid, why not ask him? I'll give him a message...'

Claribel screamed, 'Get to hell out of here.'

## 36

After Betty's exit, Claribel lay thinking for a little while longer. Betty's attack had not so much upset her as decided her: this life was ended, the one fact that Betty had revealed to her was enough to make that clear. Marcus had overheard gossip about her: this in itself was nothing. She could have got round him in some way, if that had been all. Again, his having deserted her for an evening and attached himself to another woman meant little; the evening would pass, the princess would go, Claribel would come into her own again. It was the connexion between these two things, Marcus' overhearing and Marcus' unusual behaviour, that frightened Claribel; and when you added to these, first that what he had overheard was true, and second, that the other woman was Lucy, the sum was ineluctable. Marcus was lost. Well, let him go. Claribel intended to waste no time in regrets, now that she had faced the worst. After all, Gilbert's remark, that twelve years is a long time, cut both ways...

But it meant that Gilbert must go, too. Never could she tolerate Gilbert without Marcus. She must get rid of him before he harmed her or drove her mad. She had no need of him, really, in fact he was a drag on her and her career. The rest of them didn't count; once she got away, she would never think of any of them again. She would have liked to pay out Markakis; but perhaps the chance would come later.

Where should she go? Away from London, out of England, at any rate for a time. She could not bear the thought of running into these people at every show... The idea round which her mind was cautiously circling waited until she should acknowledge its existence; if she had had to portray this process symbolically, she would have given it the shape of a woman, mysteriously smiling, sitting on the Delphic stone... Cautiously she approached it, questioned it...

'Could I go with them? Would they take me? Or at least, would they allow me to follow?' She thought of the beautiful city that was now their home, of its winding river, its majestic bridges, its squares and palaces and churches; of its people and their strange language, which she would have to learn; of its wine and music, and even its food. A new life! And if *they* would sponsor her, a brilliant career, social and artistic; money, love, fame. Marvellous! She longed to pack her trunk and go at once, without waiting to explain. If only they'd take her, how easy that would make the journey... But of course there would be too many difficulties. Her passport was in order, but she would have to get a visa. Oh, the tiresome formalities that clog the footsteps of inspiration! Oh, for the wings of a dove! Even if the worst befell, and they would not take her up again and admit her into their society, she would still go. They could not prevent her. She would do without their influence, and make her way on her own merits. Her name was sufficiently well known to be its own introduction. She could almost force her way in, on the strength of the portrait. They could not refuse to let her finish it, or pretend that they had not commissioned and sat for it. It could become a national possession, hung prominently in their art gallery. She chose for it a place on the wall, at the head of the first flight of the great wide stairs, before they divided right and left to the upper rooms. It was, or would be, good. One coronet would lead to another... And think, when there was a royal wedding! One of them was bound to marry soon; their position demanded it, their advisers would insist. Claribel, on the spot, famous already, would reap a golden harvest. And she would not be prostituting her art: in their country, pageantry was still magnificently alive. Meanwhile, apart from her public work, she would be busy collecting faces. There if anywhere in the world she would find the perfect human face she was seeking. But she would work for their country; she would propagandize. She would interest England, get loans floated, explain their wrongs… Even Ursula would be content. But it was no use approaching Ursula first, although she was the eldest and nominally the ruler; and Theresa was, of course, too young… Claribel, renewed, full of energy and courage, jumped off the bed and began attending to her appearance.

## 37

Claribel was all smiles as she stood under the light by the fireplace, and suggested to her guests that as it was nearly midnight, and some of them had to leave shortly after, it would be a good thing if they played off their remaining game of murder-party, if they wanted to, if not, of course, let them dance. But she had thought that at midnight they would want to assemble and sing 'Auld Lang Syne'. She still wore black silk trousers and a white shirt: and she looked even younger, fresher, and more charming than when the evening had begun. She counted on their wanting to play this stupid game – surely some of them would want to kiss or kick one another for the last time in the dark – and she favoured the idea, for she had no intention of taking part; and it was the best way of getting Lucy alone, without anyone's noticing their absence. All she feared was that they would be by this time too much engrossed in their dancing, and unwilling to make the effort. She would find it difficult to detach Lucy from the ever-watchful Ursula; and she herself could scarcely disappear again without arousing comment, especially as Gilbert had now come downstairs, and was standing behind her like a sinister jailer. Markakis was at his elbow. It is queer how people guess when you particularly wish to escape them; and with what cunning they arrange to thwart you without appearing to do so, though at other times you can be absent for hours and no notice is taken. Claribel was aware that there were forces arrayed against her, and the prospect of a battle of wits thrilled her.

Her suggestion had come as a surprise. Everybody had forgotten Marcus' suggestion. The room had stopped dancing; but the couples had not separated, though they had turned to hear what Claribel wished to say. They stood poised, as if waiting until she finished, so that they might turn back to each other and continue the interrupted communion. Even Marcus looked surprised, and by no means eager. His ruddy face caught the light from the strip above Claribel's head, as he gazed at her, trying to fathom her motive. By instinct, he did nothing to help her scheme, though formerly he had engineered it. When she opposed it, it had seemed to his advantage; now that she furthered it, he was sure it was not. It was touch and go. If the guests didn't show any eagerness, Claribel could not press them; she knew better than to try. She was so intent on her purpose that if the most convenient way failed, she could easily invent another. She waited, smiling. Usually, Gilbert, divining her wish, would have done the rest. But he too was silent. The wireless still played on, marking the rhythm, inviting them to return to the dance... But Claribel, though she could do no more, held them with her smile. As she slowly surveyed them, her look came to rest on Ursula; she didn't know why, except that Ursula did not seem to be so closely linked up with a partner as were the others. One couldn't see who her partner had been. Claribel continued to look at her, and her look became a question. Ursula, perfectly aware of this, answered at last, quietly:

'We think it would be charming...' Her voice trailed away into silence. She looked at her sister Lucy, who responded with a quick nod, none too gracious, Claribel thought. The youngest sister wasn't even listening. She had been absorbed in a silent conversation, of glances and smiles only, with Sylens. His lips, by now, were almost touching her forehead, and if she had looked up again, they would have touched her lips. But she did not.

'But we shall have to leave immediately after,' murmured Ursula. 'Would you please tell the chauffeur?' Claribel nodded to Gilbert; he went out. The spell was broken. Claribel clapped her hands.

'Come on, then – a last game. Markakis, please hand round the basket.' The dancers parted; the pairs were broken up, and talk became general, as Markakis went round with the lots. By the time that Gilbert returned it was all settled. The lot of detective had fallen on Dione and George. Actually, Dione had picked it, but George would not leave her. Claribel, relieved that Lucy had been spared, was only too happy to agree.

The lights were turned out. The confusion at the door, as they all filed out, would have been amusing to a spectator who knew the facts; for almost everyone was hanging back, trying to fall in behind his or her prey. By now they were beginning to enter again into the spirit of the thing. They remembered the opportunities afforded, that they hadn't taken full advantage of before; they remembered that this would be their last chance, for they were all aware that, however long the party went on, it would not be the same when the three sisters had left them. The fun, the excitement would have gone out of it. Those who remained would probably sit round the fire and talk, unless Claribel, seized with one of her fits of psychic fatigue, sent them all home early.

Claribel, falling in behind Lucy, called out softly, 'Don't make it too short, murderer. Let's have a good long-drawn out one.'

She had had less difficulty than she expected, when manoeuvring for this position; she had expected to have to edge in between Lucy and Marcus. But Marcus for some reason had hung back. Claribel smiled, to think of him feeling in people's pockets for the lost dagger. All that seemed very far away and childish. She did not know who had it, and she no longer cared. She followed, pressed close against Lucy by the person behind her; she was waiting for the moment when she could lay a hand on Lucy's arm and draw her aside up the stairs and along the dark corridor to her room. She felt very affectionate towards Lucy, who was to be for her the giver of so much good fortune. Lucy was smaller than she; she rested her two hands on Lucy's waist, ready to move her away out of the procession...

The door closed. The darkness was complete.

## 38

Theresa and Sylens were the last to join in the file. They had come to earth just in time to realize that the game had started, and the rest of the procession was almost through the door before they took their places.

Marcus had not followed Lucy; he had let the others go ahead of him; and now, when Theresa and Sylens fell in behind, he detached himself once again. Theresa went ahead; Sylens eagerly followed. But before he could get, through the door Marcus had seized his arm.

'Sylens: a minute,' he said softly.

Sylens looked up, startled.

'Look here,' said Marcus. 'I know you have that dagger. Will you give it to me and save all the fuss? It was I who dropped it, you know, and the lady wants it back, naturally. You would be getting me out of a stupid mess if you'd be a good fellow and hand it over.'

Sylens, always reasonable, listened with a rather worried look.

'Of course, old man,' he said. 'I'd like to. I understand your position. The only thing is –' He nodded ahead where Theresa was; the door was still open, and they could see the faint glimmer of her frock as she receded.

'Oh, I'll put that right,' said Marcus. 'I'll speak to her sister. Do me the favour; and I shan't forget it.'

'All right,' said Sylens, dubiously. 'Of course I would have returned it long ago if I had known just how.' Marcus, watching him, saw his impatience to be after Theresa, not to waste a precious second of the all-too-short time; and he knew that he had won. Sylens' hand went to his breast-pocket.

His hand jerked. He looked up, dumbfounded.

'Good God!' he said. 'It's gone!'

'Gone!' Marcus, unable to stand on ceremony, thrust his big hand inside Sylens' jacket. 'You're sure it was there?' He satisfied himself with a few rapid pats that the dagger had not slipped through into the lining, then, with a slap on the back, he sent Sylens after Theresa, through the door.

'Someone has forestalled us,' he said softly, as he closed the door and followed the others. 'I wonder what that means.'

## 39

The guests obediently groped their way about the darkened house, along corridors, up and down stairs, in and out of doorways. There were sounds of stumbling, and an occasional exclamation; but there was no laughter or talking, no sudden rushes and tumbles; compared with the earlier games, this one was strangely quiet. By now each had his or her preoccupation, and this was magnified by the thought that quite soon the party would be ending. The old year, too, had almost run its course; what would the new year bring? New opportunities, a new freedom, a new self maybe! The human passion for dramatizing its own inventions held them in thrall. From behind the closed door the music of the wireless was faintly audible. Dione and George, used to it as an accompaniment to their absorption in each other, had not bothered to turn it off.

Claribel, now that it was safe to do so — for the others had dispersed, and in any case, the darkness was quite impenetrable — steered Lucy gently past the head of the stairs and down the corridor to her own room. Lucy did not resist or protest; she had turned round once, as if inquiringly, but Claribel had pressed her hands reassuringly oh Lucy's waist, and she was close enough to her for Lucy to tell, if she was observant, that it was Claribel, from her clothes and her perfume. No word was spoken as they went down the long corridor. When they reached the door, Claribel held it open for Lucy to pass through; and she paused a moment and looked back, not in order to see, for that was not possible unless she first switched on the light of the room, but in order to hear if anyone were following them. Even hearing would be difficult, for the corridor was thickly carpeted; but when the ears are sharpened by acute attention, the faintest rustle, the sound of a sleeve brushing the wall, may become audible. She was unwilling to switch on any lights until they got inside, for if she did, then she and Lucy became visible. However, she discerned nothing. She followed Lucy and closed the door.

Lucy waited, standing in the middle of the room, until Claribel had found her way to the lamp at the bed's head. Then, at Claribel's invitation, she sat down on the only chair in the room, which Claribel placed for her. Claribel herself took up a position, half-sitting, half-lying, as she liked to do, on the bed. Propping herself up with cushions, she leaned on her elbow and gazed at Lucy with a smile meant to be friendly and sincere, with a mixture of playfulness. She met with no response. Lucy, her hands folded in her lap, stared away from her with unrelaxing gravity.

'Forgive me,' began Claribel, 'for bringing you here.' As Lucy did not answer, she went on a little more rapidly, 'I couldn't resist trying to get a word with you alone. You and I used to be friends; and our parting was so odd and unsatisfactory. I wanted a chance to explain.'

'There is no need,' murmured Lucy; but Claribel continued.

'Of course I know that things are very different now. In fact, to be candid, I was surprised that you were still willing to know me. I didn't expect such an honour.'

'We never forget,' said Lucy, 'our friends.'

'I see.' Claribel, pleased though she was, found herself a little puzzled also. Until now she had not given this problem more than a few passing thoughts. It had seemed to her that their acceptance of her invitation was a further proof that the past was forgotten, in so far as there was anything unpleasant to forget. But now that she had Lucy before her, so near to her, separated from her sisters, that charming profile, that smooth dark hair, those small-boned, loosely folded hands jogged her memory. Claribel's visual memory was like an obstinate, over-truthful second person sitting inside her, correcting her general memory, which was apt to be vague, especially over questions of her own conduct, and could always be won over to Claribel's point of view by a little false reasoning. Her visual memory was like the candid relative who sits silent while one tells one's most effective story, until the end, and then breaks in with a quiet reminder which spoils the point. Truly, Lucy was no weakling; it was not in her to forget an injury; even if she might, after weighing everything, forgive it. But first she would pass judgement. Claribel returned to that thought. And – if truth must be heeded – what was there to be said for Claribel? She had sold her friend to a worthless little cad of a seducer, for nothing at all; and as if that were not bad enough, he had turned out to be a spy, an enemy of Lucy's race, from whom she would have been in danger of kidnapping, perhaps death, if she had not had such good watchers to protect her. She owed no thanks to Claribel for her present safety, her restored title, her future power.

Claribel shifted uneasily on her cushions. The worst of it was, curiosity burned within her, and she didn't know how to put her question without making an admission which was probably quite unnecessary. She said:

'Was it very exciting, your life after you left Paris? I mean, your restoration – was there any bloodshed?'

'Oh no,' said Lucy mildly. 'There was a change of government, and we were recalled. Everything was quite peaceful, for us; there was no actual fighting. We could not prevent a certain amount of private revenge. That always happens when there is a revolution.'

Claribel gazed, fascinated, at this small person, so brave, so determined, on whose head so much hope, so much devotion, so much loyalty rested. It crossed her mind to wish that Lucy had been her father's only child, so that she need not share her privilege.

'Well, what will happen next?' said Claribel. 'Which of you is really the ruler? Or do you share?'

'The people wait,' said Lucy, 'to find out our wishes. And we have our advisers – ministers, men who served my father. We can't all govern. The question is, which of us shall carry on the line? There is no law of primogeniture in our country. Of course, the matter is virtually decided among us three.'

'Is it you?' said Claribel, eagerly. 'I hope so.'

'That is kind of you,' said Lucy, calmly. 'I'm sure you mean it kindly, though actually, I assure you, you are mistaken: it is good fortune to escape the position. And that good fortune will be mine. The choice lies between my two sisters. I am exempt – thanks, in a way, to you.' Her voice had not changed, but the words startled Claribel.

'What do you mean?' she said, rather falteringly. 'Thanks to me? What have I got to do with it?'

Lucy turned for the first time and looked at her. 'A great deal,' she said, clearly. Claribel quailed. 'And since you have brought me here, I may as well tell you.' She stood up. She had no need of height to enhance her dignity. 'Do you know why I came here this evening? I came to kill you.' Her voice was impersonal, cold, meditative: she looked at Claribel as if she were a joint of meat from which she was wondering where she could cut the first slice. 'It seemed to me unfair that *you* should escape the fate of your fellow-conspirator.

*He* foolishly walked into the net; *you* just as foolishly rose to the bait. I made my sister Ursula agree to come here. Naturally, I didn't explain why. But I imagine it was not necessary.'

It is to be placed to the credit of Claribel that physical fear was not one of her weaknesses. What was preoccupying her now was not Lucy's intent to kill – though she did not doubt it – but the desire to keep her there a little longer. She wished to hear more. She was more interested than she had been for years; here at last was a dramatic situation, a romantic personality, such as she was always seeking and scarcely ever found. She acknowledged in her heart an affinity between Lucy and Marcus: he, too, would kill, if he so decided, coolly and without remorse.

'Then why,' she said, leaning forward, 'didn't you kill me if that was what you thought? What made you change your mind?'

Lucy looked sharply down at her; and for a moment, Claribel wondered if she had been too quick in assuming her safety. Before Lucy could answer, she went on rapidly, 'I admit I brought you and Raymond together. Also, I admit he wasn't worthy. But I swear to you that I didn't know he was a spy. I thought–'

'You thought it would be a pleasant experience for me. I know. Well, I was saved from that by the vigilance of others. But, you see, I was not saved from the breath of scandal. Others had to be let into the secret. There are waiting-women, and men too, who talk. And so, to the ladies of the court, I am, at best, the very indiscreet *jeune fille* who was saved by a miracle from smirching my ancient name; at worst – and believe me, court ladies would rather assume the worst, especially when the setting is Paris – I am the mistress of a traitor, perhaps a traitor myself. They envy me the supposed love adventure. As for the rest, they daren't say – not now. But let me tell you that if our friends had failed, it would have been not least because *I* gave our enemies a weapon against us: anything will do to inflame popular opinion. Your protégé was shot: there are still people who mutter that it was because he knew too much about our private lives when we were in exile – for my sisters were included in my disgrace. My sisters say nothing. Theresa is too young. Ursula is too wise. But believe me, if I had done what I intended, neither of them would blame me at all.'

She drew her short fur coat round her, as if she had been paying a call and the correct time to end the visit was at hand. Claribel, still afraid of losing her, cried out eagerly:

'Don't go, don't go. What you say is terrible.' Actually she was thrilled to find that any action of hers could have consequences so far-reaching; she felt herself at last in the main current of European intrigue; and she longed to hear more. 'I didn't know. I was your friend. I thought Raymond was harmless. Well, poor boy, he has paid for his crime. Isn't that enough? Can't we let bygones be bygones and be friends again?' She had not forgotten her main objective. She felt that time was passing quickly; at any moment they might hear the scream which meant that the game was ended, and she didn't wish the others to know that she had abstracted Lucy; she must get her out of the room before the lights went up. Whoever had picked the lot of murderer had certainly obeyed her injunction to make it a good long game. She gazed up at Lucy, using all her childlike innocence and charm.

'Don't be afraid,' said Lucy, contemptuously, 'you have nothing to fear from me. The moment has gone by, and I am no longer interested.' She began walking to the door.

Claribel was offended. She would rather be the object of hatred, even murderous hatred, than of indifference. She said quickly, to Lucy's back:

'You haven't told me why you changed your mind.'

But Lucy's hand was already on the door.

'Perhaps,' added Claribel, 'you lost your weapon – or gave it away.'

Lucy, the door half-open, paused, but without turning; but only for a moment. Claribel, satisfied that she had planted her sting, gave up the attempt to detain her. And as always with Claribel, now that the uselessness of any further effort had become certain, she instantly ceased to think about it; she did not even bother to take a last look at Lucy as she disappeared into the dark corridor, nor at the door as it slowly closed behind her. Instead, she rolled over on to her stomach on the bed, and dismissed the three princesses for ever from her life. The interview had been refreshing; it had cured her of her vapours. How absurd her idea had been, that it was necessary to leave Gilbert! Never, never would she forsake him, tower of strength that he was, and venture forth into the cynical, hostile world, so harsh in its judgements, so impervious to the arguments and overtures of Claribel. As for Marcus, let him go if he wanted to. She and Gilbert would get on very well alone.

She began planning a sea cruise that they would take down the Mediterranean, among the Aegean Islands, perhaps to Asia Minor and Egypt this spring. Beside her bed, on the table, was a book about Minoan Crete, given her by Markakis. She stretched out her hand for it, and propping it up on the pillows, began turning the pages. The drawings and photographs interested, absorbed her: their art – how exquisite, how fine, how different from all other! Her problems, her interview with Lucy, all thought of the future, were obliterated. She forgot that it must be nearly midnight, and still no one had screamed.

The door began opening again. Claribel, lying full length on the bed, her back turned, one of her silk-clad legs bent upwards at the knee and swinging gently, her chin propped in her hands, heard and saw nothing.

## 40

Markakis, with sure instinct, had picked on Claribel and Lucy to follow. He had drawn the lot of murderer: he knew which it was, and he had snatched it out first, before the tray went round. In this way he made certain that the game would not end until he so decided; and he wished to walk round a bit and see if he could discover what each of the actors in his play were up to, and how the intrigue was working itself out. He also liked the sensation of power; he was like Destiny itself, since he could slit the thin-spun thread of this evening's final game, or prolong it, as he felt inclined.

He had been at once aware of Claribel's designs on Lucy; he was immediately behind Lucy, having intended to keep near her, when Claribel pushed in between them; and he was aware, as Claribel's elbows pressed back against him, that she was steering Lucy along in the procession, waiting for the moment when she could detach her. It was as he expected: at the top of the stairs Claribel held Lucy to one side while the others dispersed. Markakis too stood against the wall and waited. When he heard them moving again, he had no need to follow: he knew the way to Claribel's room. So he stood in the shadows at the stair head and waited; then, when Claribel's door had closed, he had quickly followed down the corridor, stepping sideways into recesses and doorways at the slightest sound, until he got as close as he could. And as he listened, all thought of other developments, Theresa and Sylens, Ursula and Carraway, Marcus and his quest for the dagger, was submerged. He had been right;

he had picked on the central theme of the drama, to which all the others were sidelines. That he was eavesdropping did not trouble him; his standards were quite unmoral, and he would have thought it a sin to neglect such a feast for the imagination as the gods had laid before him. He listened, his ears tingling, his eyes occasionally narrowing, and sometimes he smiled, or rather, bared his teeth, at the revelation of the characters of Lucy and Claribel. He would not have sold his place for a seat on Olympus...

When Lucy opened the door he shrank back into the shadows. Her coat sleeve touched his hand as she went by. The door closed again. There seemed no reason for staying. Yet he stayed, to make sure that she had really gone. He was still there when he heard the faint rustle of another frock as it brushed the wall; someone else – or was it Lucy again? – was coming this way. Again he flattened himself back, and again the sleeve of a fur coat brushed his hand. As the door was pushed slowly ajar, and the subdued light fell on the face of the intruder, he saw that it was not Lucy, but Ursula.

Minutes passed. Perhaps it was only seconds. Markakis, dominated as if from outside by an inability to move, closed his eyes. He heard, he heard, and nothing more. Apart from this terrible sense of hearing, which was vividly, violently awake, he was barely conscious. The wall supported him; his feet were embedded in the carpet, else he would have slipped to the ground. There were no words, no cry, only – sounds.

Thus Markakis took his revenge on Claribel, for, petrified as he was, there was within him a clear knowledge of what bound him: it was a purpose, as reckless, as terrible as Ursula's. He had chosen. His brain worked furiously...

When Ursula came out, she had scarcely passed him by when he roused himself and followed her. She turned like a tiger. If she had still had the dagger in her hand – but he stopped her instantly.

'Go on,' he whispered. 'I follow you. Get near the others. I am the murderer. I put my hands round your throat. Count thirty or forty, then scream. I slip out to get your chauffeur. You are safe. Hurry.'

'But the dagger?' said Ursula. 'You are one of us? You take this on yourself? You are under orders?'

'The dagger has passed through many hands.'

'I know.'

'Hurry then.'

Cautiously they began creeping down the stairs.

The scream rang out. The lights went up. George and Dione, somewhat slow to arrive, found Ursula lying across the floor of the cellar, where most of the party seemed to have collected. Lucy was there, and Sylens and Theresa; Carraway brooded sitting on a cask in one corner, Marcus drifted in from somewhere near by: smiling across at Lucy, he shook his head and showed his empty hands. Markakis leaned against the jamb of the door.

Dione and George, bored at the interruption, scarcely pretended to look round. The party began to file back to the ground-floor sitting-room; they were cold, and tired of waiting: there were complaints at the length of time taken by the murderer. It was clear that all the fun had gone out of the game, and that the detection was not going to prove interesting, even if anybody troubled to carry it out. Upstairs the guests began filling their glasses; nobody looked in the mood to answer questions, and George and Dione were obviously incapable of asking any. The wireless still played, but no one made a move to dance. The three sisters stood together by the fire waiting.

'Where's Gilbert?' murmured someone. 'Where's Claribel?' murmured someone else; but nobody bothered to reply. It was nearly midnight; the last two dance tunes were announced; but even this didn't rouse the utterly dampened party.

Markakis appeared on the threshold, and behind him a man in livery.

'Your chauffeur wants to speak to you, madam,' he said to Ursula. 'It seems that a telephone message has come from the aerodrome: you have to leave at once.' The man came forward and bowed. Ursula led the way out of the room. Her sisters followed. So too did Marcus and Sylens; but Carraway stayed at the sideboard, drinking; and Markakis stayed where he was, leaning against the door.

Outside, in the lane, there were cries of 'Goodbye!' as the car moved silently, stealthily, powerfully away. Peggy, peering out through the curtains said, 'That's funny: I don't see Claribel there.'

Desmond, squeezing her waist, said, 'She leaves all that sort of thing to Gilbert, don't you know.'

Peggy said, 'I don't see him either. But then, I only have eyes for you.' She giggled; he drew her against him and kissed her. Betty, sitting morose and alone on the fender, watched them. The Irishman had joined Carraway, and they were drinking whisky side by side.

'God, what a party!' said George to Dione. 'Let's go, dear. Claribel has evidently retired for the night.' They bustled away. Marcus and Sylens returned.

From the wireless set came the booming of midnight; and from outside, mingling with it, the sound of distant hooters, whistles and bells.

They all stood silent until the chimes ended.

'Well,' began Marcus, 'this is a queer way to see the New Year in. Half of the guests have gone' – he paused, but only for a moment, though even he was cracking under the strain of that parting, for God knew how long – 'and our host and hostess are absent. By the way, what has become of the two detectives? Have they flown?'

Nobody would play up to him. Sylens walked away without speaking; Markakis, pale and abstracted, did not seem to hear. Carraway and the Irishman had their backs turned. Betty, sitting on the fender, was negligible. Desmond and Peggy were absorbed in their flirtation. Marcus took a purposeful stride forward, as if to take one last look through the window, though the car had long since turned the corner. Then suddenly something made him turn.

Gilbert was standing in the threshold. His eyes were wide with horror, his mouth open, but no words came. He made a curious, weak gesture at Marcus...

The aeroplane was leaving England behind, heading away from the coast with its rows of lights like brilliants set on an invisible frame, out over the sea. The three sisters, warm and comfortable, sat together in the forepart, shut off from their attendants by sliding glass panes. Seen from outside, their three profiles would have looked as though superimposed in low relief, first Theresa, then Lucy, then Ursula. They were still dressed as at Claribel's party.

'It was your dagger, Lucy,' said Ursula. 'Perhaps that was too bold. But I thought it only just; and I don't think I really endangered you. Everybody knows you lost it; and it has passed through several hands. It will be an interesting problem, for the English police... *I* did not hold it in my bare hands.'

Theresa sighed. 'Oh, dear,' she said. 'I'm afraid the last bare hand that touched it was my poet's. Do you think he'll be accused, Ursula? I hope not, he was so sweet. But anyone would know it wasn't he, wouldn't they? He would only talk. He would not act, ever.'

'That doesn't apply to *my* friend,' said Lucy, sombrely. 'He has handled the dagger. And he has perhaps a motive for killing Claribel. But I have no fears for him. He would know how to extricate himself from any danger. I wouldn't mind travelling to the ends of the earth with *him*.'

'Did you like him so much?' cried Theresa, eagerly. 'Oh, Lucy, how delightful. I didn't know you ever could be weak.'

Lucy smiled. 'I trusted him,' she said. 'That's the finest feeling one can have about another person. It's better than love.'

'Were you sorry to say goodbye to him?' Theresa pressed her. 'Do you think you will ever see him again?'

Lucy thought; but she could not utter her thoughts to Theresa. She could not say, 'But for me and my momentary weakness, long ago, you, dear child, wouldn't be heading for a royal consort and a throne' – for she and Ursula had privately agreed that it was to be Theresa – nor could she declare her own determination to retire as soon as that happened, and marry whom she pleased. She longed for that day, when she could be a citizen of the world, and not the Princess Lucy, bearer of an ancient name. As for Ursula's plans, she did not know them; but Ursula would never relinquish power: she would stay, the virtual ruler, the hand behind Theresa's throne… All Lucy said in answer to Theresa's question was, 'That is left to him.'

'And you trust him!' laughed Theresa. Lucy did not say no.

Ursula, only half listening to her sisters' conversation, had been pursuing her own thoughts. Her rich voice broke in gravely.

'It was strange about the boy Markakis.'

'Why?' said Lucy, interested. Markakis had made an impression on her: she saw him still, his dark lock of hair, his brooding eyes; she heard his music.

'You realize that he saved me – saved us all? If any questions are asked about us, it is he who will see to it that we are not pestered. You know that he followed me: that he listened outside the door? And then, when I came out, he told me what to do? He will swear that he was with me all the time – that I never left the basement. He saved me, certainly. I wonder why. I wondered if he were – one of us: if he were put there by our friends. I don't know. I am puzzled.'

'He knew who we were,' murmured Lucy. 'He recognized us. He promised to send me some music which he was going to compose about us.'

'Do you think they will accuse *him*?' said Theresa.

'I was wondering,' said Ursula, thoughtfully. 'I don't think they would have proof. *His* finger-marks aren't on the dagger; and if he swears he followed *me*, and I were to corroborate that, I doubt whether they'd realize that our two statements stood or fell together. I think he is capable of wriggling out of it. If he does, we shall see *him* again.'

'That will be lovely!' cried Theresa.

'Yes,' said Lucy, 'it will be interesting to hear him play his music. I think I gathered, even in the few minutes he talked to me, that for some reason he hated Claribel.'

'That,' said Ursula, 'is not strange.'

They fell silent. Below them the sea tossed, dark and restless; above, a million stars glittered. They flew between, calm as goddesses, untouched by even a breath of wind.

## 45

Claribel lay face downwards on the bed. The handle of Lucy's dagger stuck out from between her shoulder-blades, and round the hilt, on her white silk shirt, was a red stain. Her face was pressed against the book she had been reading.

Marcus, Markakis, and Gilbert stood round; Sylens was in the doorway.

'Those women!' snarled Gilbert. 'It was one of them. It must have been. What was all that rot you were telling me, Markakis, about this dagger? It belonged to one of them. Which?'

'The dagger,' said Markakis, 'belonged to the Princess Lucy. But she lost it, earlier in the evening, or rather, gave it away.'

'Yes,' Marcus corroborated, 'she gave it to me.'

'You!' Gilbert wheeled round.

'Yes,' Markakis recalled him. 'Don't you remember? I told you. And then he quarrelled with Claribel—'

'Ah!' Gilbert wheeled round on Marcus again, 'he quarrelled with her.'

'And she,' Markakis went on imperturbably, 'got the dagger away from him. She thought it was a love gift, and she threw it out of the window. I saw it fall.'

'You seem to have seen a good deal,' said Gilbert. 'You picked it up, perhaps?'

'No,' said Markakis, 'I did not touch it. As you see, I am not wearing gloves. Get it examined for finger-prints. You will find the

Princess Lucy's, of course, as it is hers; and Marcus's above those, and above those, others perhaps – but not mine.'

Gilbert glowered at him, baffled. 'Nor mine either,' he said. The remark struck them as strange. For the first time, they wondered if the loss of Claribel was going to prove as devastating to Gilbert as they had feared. Markakis continued:

'At that moment Sylens and the Princess Theresa happened to pass that way. She recognized the dagger, and gave it to Sylens. Beyond that, I know nothing.'

Sylens' voice came faintly from the doorway. 'Yes, that's true. I had it all through supper, and while we were dancing. Then Marcus came and asked me for it, just before the game; and I found it had gone.'

'The game!' snarled Gilbert. 'The murder-game!'

'Remember,' put in Markakis, 'that the last game was suggested by Claribel.'

'Yes,' said Gilbert, 'but not in the first instance. Upstairs, it was suggested by Marcus.'

'That's true,' said Marcus. 'I hoped for a chance to find the dagger and give it back to its owner.'

'Who were you dancing with?' said Gilbert to Sylens. 'Theresa, of course.'

'Yes.'

'Then she must have taken it from you.'

'You're not suggesting, are you,' said Markakis, 'that she killed Claribel?'

'She didn't,' said Sylens, in a low voice. 'All through that last game she never left me, not for a second. We were in the basement the whole time.'

'So was Lucy,' murmured Marcus.

'So was Ursula,' added Markakis, with a quick glance at Marcus. Each recognized the other's lie, and pledged himself to support it.

'Well, you were the last who had it,' snarled Gilbert. 'When did *you* lose it? How?'

'I don't know,' said Sylens, wearily. 'I wandered out into the garden for a minute. Perhaps I dropped it then.'

Gilbert cast a look of hatred at all three.

'You lie!' he said. 'You lie! I shall go for the police.' He ran out of the room.

The three stared at each other across Claribel's body.

'You don't think *he* did it, do you?' said Marcus.

'No,' answered Markakis, 'but he *could* have, and he knows it. That's why he is so keen to fix the real guilt on someone. Until then, he'll feel morally guilty, you see. He had good reason to hate Claribel.'

There was a silence. In the distance they heard the tinkle of the telephone bell as Gilbert lifted the receiver.

'Well, gentlemen,' said Marcus, 'I think we all know our parts?'